Lover's Bid

WELCOME TO
Southlake Park

BACHELOR
AUCTION
IN PROGRESS

A.C. ARTHUR

DISTINGUISHED GENTLEMEN

An Artistry Publishing Book
LOVER'S BID,
First Edition: 2019
Copyright © 2019 by A.C. Arthur
All rights reserved.

www.acarthur.net

This book is a work of fiction. Characters, names, locations, events and incidents (in either a contemporary and/or historical setting) are products of the author's imagination and are being used in an imaginative manner as a part of this work of fiction. Any resemblance to actual events, locations, settings or persons, living or dead, is entirely coincidental.

LOVER'S BID

They were the best of friends in college but after going off into the world their lives drastically changed. Now, Dylan James, in-house counsel for a D.C. lobbyist firm is once again face-to-face with Cristine Palmer, defense attorney from New York. The passion that had been on a low simmer because of prior relationships is now on full blast. But Dylan has a dark side that he's certain Cristine will not understand. Cristine has not come this far to walk away from her feelings for Dylan again, so following him to Chicago and bidding for the lover she's always dreamed of is her only option.

FOREWORD

Dear Reader,

This novella is part of the Distinguished Gentlemen Series. It is 1 of 14 novellas that are connected by an event—The Southlake Park Bachelor Auction which will take place live during the Book Euphoria Weekend Block Party.

Here is a list of all the books in this series:

- *The Alpha Bid* by Ty Young
- *The Rival Bid* by Reese Ryan
- *The Reluctant Bid by Sheryl Lister*
- *Losing the Bid* by Suzette Riddick
- *Invitation to Bid by Angela Seals*
- *The Contingency Bid by Sherelle Green*
- *The Renegade Bid by Kelsey Green*
- *The Birthday Bid by Suzette D. Harrison*
- *An Outlandish Bid by E.J. Brock*
- *A Bid on Forever by Joy Avery*
- *Switched at Bid* by Nicole Falls

- *The Closing Bid by Elle Wright*
- *The Bid Catcher by Anita Davis*

Each novella can be read as a standalone, so please do not feel as if you are committed to purchasing and reading each novella in the series. However, I can safely say that you might be missing out on 14 fantastic stories if you don't.

As always, I hope you enjoy Dylan and Cristine's story and wish you very happy reading!

AC

Chicago

They were bidding on men, bachelors to be more specific.

A room full of women, obviously with money to spend, were sitting on the edge of their seats eager and ready to make their winning bids.

Cris had no idea what she'd gotten herself into. The only thing she knew was that she'd left New York looking for something to fill a void that had been building within her for the last few years. Instead of heading back to South Carolina where she'd been born, Cris had gone to another familiar place, Washington D.C. To be precise, she'd gone to Dylan James. He had been the best thing about her years in D.C. and Cris thought he might be the key to what she felt her life was missing.

A series of strange events had taken place in the two days she'd been in D.C. and now, Cris was in Chicago at the

Southlake Park Cultural Center. She was seated at a table near the back, staring down at a program that matched the brochure she'd found near Dylan's car at the parking garage in D.C. Yes, she'd really hopped on a train to see this man in D.C. and then bought a plane ticket to follow him to Chicago.

Crazy?

Hell yes!

Worth it?

Well, she was about to find out because Dylan James a.k.a. The Master had just stepped onto the stage. The bidding and whatever was meant to happen next, was about to begin.

The Next Night
Washington, D.C.

"I want you to strip, insert the gag and lay on your stomach across the bed. I'll bind your hands and fuck you until I'm done."

Cris resisted the urge to gasp and curse. But yeah, she really had some choice words running through her mind at this very moment. For starters, who the hell did he think he was? No, who the hell did he think *she* was? More importantly, did he just say gag and bind?

In all fairness, she was the one who followed him to Chicago after he'd walked out on her at the club in D.C. She was also the one who stood in a room full of women and bid four thousand seven hundred and fifty dollars—almost every penny of her personal savings—to secure one night with the man who had once been her best friend.

But she was not a prostitute or some sort of sex slave which was exactly how his tersely spoken instructions made her seem. In fact, Cristine Angela Palmer graduated summa cum laude from Howard University and in the top 2% from Syracuse Law School. She was a twenty-nine year old corporate attorney with a 2.5 million dollar trust fund that her parents started when shew as born but Cris had never touched. And she was presently standing in a brightly lit room debating whether or not she'd made a colossal mistake.

"Wouldn't it be more romantic if we had some candlelight and music? We could undress each other and then—"

"That's not how this works," he interrupted and turned to lock the front door. "You bid on a night in my playroom. We're here and we'll get started."

Right. Cris nodded but she was almost positive there had been nothing in that brochure from the Southlake Bachelor Auction that described her being bound, gagged and fucked. However, she had known exactly who she was dealing with when she'd made the first bid. That wasn't entirely accurate. Cris knew Dylan James, the college student. As for the man Dylan had become, well, she had a feeling she was about to get a crash course in just who that was.

"I don't do romance. You paid for tonight. I intend to give you what you paid for." He walked to the other end of the space and stopped at a desk. Reaching into the front pocket of his pants he pulled out a silver key ring with only a few keys attached. He unlocked the top drawer of the desk and pulled out some papers.

"I've stated what I want," he told her when he was once again standing in front of her. "The consent agreement says you understand that and give your permission to participate. There's nothing in here regarding the terms of the auction, but that was covered in the bill of sale you received once your credit card payment was processed in Chicago. Sign and date on page three and we'll begin."

Cris accepted the stapled pages without looking at them. Instead, her gaze remained riveted on Dylan's chocolate brown eyes. When had they become so hardened and serious? He was still tall with an almond complexion, close cut hair and goatee. And he still wore a suit just as well as casual attire and appeared sexier than any man she'd ever seen.

"If you need a pen there are some in the holder on the desk. I'll give you a few minutes to look over the agreement and ask any questions you may have."

His next words were spoken in a tone that said he was willing to answer questions, but really hoped it wasn't necessary. After all, they were both attorneys. Cris knew her way around a contract. She'd started her career at a large firm where she handled defense litigation for insurance companies and then progressed to the firm's corporate department, so her last few years had been filled with contracts, agreements and pleadings designed to circumvent or enforce them all.

But this was an agreement to allow him to perform sexual acts with her.

Sex with Dylan.

Her body was definitely on board for that.

Her mind, however, overruled and she took a few moments to review every word. From aftercare and anal training to soft limit and voyeurism there was a complete vocabulary that correlated with the terms of the agreement which comprised the final three pages of the six-page document. Cris wasn't totally familiar with them all, but reading women's fiction and erotica novels was one of her favorite forms of de-stressing and so she knew a little bit about...this situation.

What she'd never known or saw coming was that Dylan was a part of this world. Cris looked up after reading the last word.

He was once again moving across the room—the extremely dour looking room. The furniture definitely looked expensive so that wasn't the problem. The bare smoke gray-painted walls and glossed cement floors gave a very cold and uniform aura. This was a studio apartment, but it had been designed to look like one huge bedroom. The bed with its four metal posts shooting up to within inches of the ceiling was positioned in the center of the space. There was a black satin duvet turned down on one side to reveal a gray sheet. No pillows.

As Cris continued to peruse the area she noted long black lacquer tables pushed against the walls on both sides of the room. On one table there was a black box with a number of drawers, the handles sparkling like diamonds. She wondered what was inside. On another table there were towels folded neatly and stacked in piles alternating between black and gray colors. Dylan removed the wool jacket he'd been wearing. He opened a stainless steel armoire and hung the jacket inside.

"Your twenty-four hour period started ten minutes ago when we walked through the door."

His tone was clipped and Cris wondered where the guy she'd stayed up with under the guise of studying so many nights had gone. Those were the memorable years that Cris perhaps foolishly thought she could recreate when she returned to D.C.

Dylan never left D.C. after grad school, but went on to attend the Francis King Carey School of Law at the University of Maryland. Cris hadn't seen or spoken to him in almost nine years.

She held up her hand and waved the contract in the air. "So we're definitely handling this like I'm a paying customer? Despite the fact that I know more about you than probably anyone else in this whole city."

Dylan had lived in a house on campus with four other guys, one of which had been Cris's boyfriend during freshman and part of sophomore year. Which was why Cris had taken Dylan's warnings about her ex seriously and ended the relationship before things became too problematic. In turn, when Cris's roommate had set her sights on Dylan, Cris had been quick to tell him that the girl was more interested in the fact that Dylan's father had just started his campaign to become a senator and that there were rumors Dylan would be following his father's footsteps. That's how they'd become friends, sharing information and commiserating together. They'd remained close depending only on each other for honesty and support until graduation.

"I'm not that guy anymore, Cris. That guy would have never gone to a place like The Corporation. I'm still not sure how you were able to get in." Dylan's brow furrowed, his dark gaze pinning her to the spot where she stood.

The Corporation was an elite sex club with facilities all over the world. Its clientele ranged from diplomats to businessman who dared to pay expansive amounts of money for the pleasure that drove everything they did or could ever imagine. Membership at The Corporation was a powerful drug, taking money from the globe's largest bank accounts to fund an age-old habit. An enterprise built by men and women with one thought in mind: pleasure. The idea had been simple, its implementation professional and high class, its profits, staggering.

"Just because I've never been to the club, doesn't mean I'd never heard of it. There's one in New York. A couple of my former clients were patrons. I called one of them and they gave me a recommendation. That, along with two hundred and fifty dollars, got me through the door. I didn't know you were such a valued member at an upscale sex club."

He stared at her as if he might say something more, maybe explain what had happened that hardened him so much over the past nine years, but he did not. He undid the buttons at his wrists and rolled up the sleeves of his shirt.

"Are you signing the agreement or not?"

He sounded as if he meant business.

Okay. Cris could slip into her lawyerly mode as well.

"Section two, clause four calls for proof of acceptable medical health. I'm not sure twenty-four hours is time enough for both of us to abide by these terms," she stated evenly. "I have a latex allergy so I travel with a personal supply of polyurethane condoms and only use water based lubricants. Also, I'm stating a resounding no to any form of whipping, spanking or torture."

For one, Cris had been raised in a house with three older brothers who loved to tease and bully her. She learned to fight back early on and hadn't stopped since. And two, whipping, spanking and torture weren't things most African Americans would tolerate in this day and age.

He stopped unbuttoning his shirt to stare at her intently. "I do not possess any whips or paddles and do not get off on torture."

"Then you might need to rewrite your consent agreement."

Cris reached into her purse and pulled out a pen. She drew a line through the clause she was opposing and scribbled her initials beside it. Just above the signature line she added a new clause detailing her latex allergy and subsequent requirements before initialing that clause as well. Closing the space between them she offered him the pen and agreement saying, "Your turn."

He didn't read what she'd written, just initialed the two places where she had and signed his name on the designated line. He crossed the room again, placed the contract in the top desk drawer and turned back to her.

"Strip."

The solitary word was spoken with chilling clarity that should not have sent tendrils of desire skating down her spine. But try as she might, Cris could not control the urgings that had been prickling her skin since the night she'd watched Dylan at The Corporation sitting in a chair while a woman gave him a hand job. Again, she shouldn't have been aroused at that sight. She hadn't thought she should have been jealous either. She and Dylan had never been a couple. Yet, a mixture of both feelings had rippled through her body with such ferocity that she'd waited outside the men's room for him to appear after cleaning himself.

But now was not the time for memories. Cris yanked the leather jacket she wore from her shoulders. She tossed it and her purse onto the bed and pulled her blouse from the ban of her jeans. He was right, she'd paid for twenty-four hours, she was going to get what she paid for, even though she had no idea what that was.

Her breasts were high, blush-colored nipples were large and hard before she bent over to push the tight jeans she wore down her long slim legs. How many times had Dylan wondered how she would look naked and bared completely to him? Too damn many.

But Cris was off limits. She was supposed to be like the sister he never had. Only Dylan was certain the dreams he'd once had nightly about her were not the way normal brothers thought of their sisters. She wasn't supposed to be here. Not tonight and certainly not a week ago when he'd gone to The Corporation expecting his regular sexual release. Yet there she was, wearing a skintight green dress and outrageously high heels. Her hair had been piled atop her head in a haphazard, yet stunningly sexy, style. Her face was made-up, her eyes wider than he recalled, lips plumper. Everything about her seemed magnified and overwhelming and Dylan recalled feeling as if he'd been punched in the gut...with a battering ram.

Some nameless woman had approached him. She was a regular at The Corporation and had serviced him before, so Dylan didn't squabble when she'd fallen to her knees and eased her way between his legs. He hadn't looked down at her either. His gaze had been locked with Cris's. So while no-name worked his cock with her hands, Cris took hold of his mind and every nerve in his body. Every reaction, from his initial erection, to the swirls of pleasure starting at his groin and spreading down to his thighs, up his spine and eventually throughout his entire body, were because of the gorgeous woman he was staring at. The woman he thought he'd never see again.

"I'm ready." Her words snapped him out of his reverie and...

Damn.

Head-to-toe creamy tawny-hued skin stood before him. In addition to the perfect breasts her mound was clean-shaven, as if she knew exactly what he required even before she'd known who and what he was.

"The gag."

Did his voice sound shaky?

Dylan turned away from her. He removed his shirt and went to one of the drawers. Running his hand over the selection of ball gags, Dylan chose the small silicone heart with the faux leather harness. It was new and the perfect size for a beginner, as if he too had somehow known the next guest in his playroom would be a novice. He was just about to turn and toss the gag to her when he felt her arms going around his waist. The gag slipped from his hand landing on the floor.

"The lady in the club didn't wait for you to give her instructions," she told him. "And you enjoyed everything she did to you."

Cris's arms moving around him were different. Dylan preferred not to be touched. To bring about sexual release was fine, but nothing intimate. Intimacy meant feelings were involved. Feelings meant some type of commitment. None of which he was interested in. Cris flattened her palms over his abs, blunt tipped nails sliding seductively over his skin as they lowered to the ban of his pants.

"I've worked with her before. She is experienced in what I require." Again, his voice sounded different. Dylan did not like it.

"Well, I have some experience in the area of sex," she said before touching her lips and the tip of her tongue to his shoulder blade.

Dylan was five feet eleven inches tall. Cris, in her bare feet, was five feet three inches of spunk and smarts. She'd come up on the tip of her toes to drop that kiss, an action that was absurdly sexy to him. Her fingers were working his belt buckle. The metal made a clanking sound when it was freed and she immediately went to the button of his slacks.

"You paid for a night in the playroom. You will do the things that are done here."

He focused on controlling the tempo of his words as well as the actions taking place. He covered her hands just as she finished with the button and unzipped his pants.

"I want you on that bed and gagged."

What Dylan really wanted was for both of them to be fully dressed and sitting in their favorite booth at Tony's Grill feasting on their favorite bacon cheeseburgers. How had he ended up here, in this room, with her? Everything about this was so wrong. But when she ignored his words and reached through the slit of his boxers to cup his now thick erection, Dylan closed his eyes to the instant jolt of pleasure.

Cris sighed, her breath warm as she rested her forehead against his back.

"I've wondered for so long," she whispered. "You've always been built. I worked out with you in the gym so your fierce muscles aren't a shock to me. But this, I've wondered how this would feel. In my hands and in my—"

"Don't." The word was sharp and ripped from him with startling force. "Not here."

There was nothing personal here. Not in this space. Everything he'd placed in this room was for his sexual release. That was all.

Again, she ignored him as if he hadn't been talking at all these past minutes. Cris always had a one-track mind. The one track being whatever it was she'd focused herself on at the moment. Right now, it appeared she was focused on making him come in her hand. She'd pulled his length free of his boxers and was now stroking up and down his rigid stalk like she was rubbing a prized pet. Her thumbs ran over the tip of his dick and his eyes rolled back in his head. He was not going to come just from her giving him a quick hand job. He was not!

"It feels better than I expected."

"I did not expect this." The admission was involuntary and he clenched his teeth with annoyance.

On the down stroke her knuckles grazed his balls and Dylan saw bursts of color behind his closed lids.

"Expect the unexpected," she whispered. "Haven't I told you that before?"

She had.

Dylan did not like surprises.

She licked his back again and pumped his dick faster.

The unexpected was about to get interesting.

2

*D*ylan turned around breaking the contact of her hand on his dick. She looked startled for a moment but then quickly stepped close to him once more.

"Lay on the bed," he told her when she was about to touch him again.

She hesitated and he repeated, "Lay on the bed."

A few seconds more and she finally went to the bed and sat. She placed her palms on the mattress behind her and scooted back slowly until she was in the center. Then she leaned back on her elbows and whispered, "Come here."

Dylan didn't move.

Although he wanted to run over and spread her legs wide. He wanted to sink deep inside of her and hold on because he knew it would be a journey that he was in no way prepared for.

Why was she here? Why had she followed him to Chicago and paid all that money for this night with him? Dammit!

He couldn't turn her away, could not renege on the agreement made between the Southlake Park Restoration

Committee and each patron of the auction. It was a binding agreement and the last thing he wanted to do to the event organizer and the woman who had been the closest thing Dylan ever had to a real grandmother, was cause her any legal troubles. Not that he thought for one instant that Cris would sue. The fact that it was a viable and winnable option, had him standing in his most private place with a raging hard on and a woman who could destroy him.

Dylan removed the rest of his clothes and shoes. He ignored the gag on the floor and walked to a cabinet. He opened the door and selected two silk ties and a small white box. He returned to the bed realizing that she was watching him. He wanted to believe that meant nothing to him. Dylan spent a good amount of his time in the gym, not so much to maintain physical attributes, but moreso to be preemptive against hereditary ailments such as high blood pressure and heart disease. Still, he was well aware of the fact that he had a perfectly sculpted body that women enjoyed seeing naked. This was Cris's first time seeing him naked. Her perusal did not feel as normal as being stared at by other women did.

Cris's body was exceptional as well. Dylan had known it would be. He'd watched her work out so many times. He'd watched her walk into and out of a room and he'd longed for her, knowing that he could never have her.

"I'm going to tie your wrists to the bedpost." He knelt on the bed and took one of her wrists in his hand.

Her skin was soft. She rolled over so that she was now on her knees and closer to him than she had been before.

"Then I won't be able to touch you like this," she said and with her free hand once again grasped his dick.

Dylan stopped, silk tie in one hand, her wrist in the other. He swallowed hard and tried to remain focused. It wasn't easy. Not this time. Not with her.

"Did you ever think of us making love?"

Her hands were magical. He could admit that to himself and not grapple further with how horribly he was failing at handling this situation. She was jerking him with swift motions that were guaranteed to make him come if he just let her continue. And damn he wanted her to continue.

"That's not what we're doing here."

"Oh yeah, it is," she replied. "I imagined reaching into your pants and doing exactly this so many times when we were studying or that time we went to the movies to see one of those action movies you love so much."

His hips moved involuntarily. Just a quick thrust into her hand and Dylan clenched his teeth so hard his temples throbbed.

"We did not have a sexual relationship," he said when he finally trusted his voice not to crack.

"But you wanted one didn't you?"

Her hand stopped moving. The quick pause in pleasure had him immediately staring down at her. She tilted her head, strands of silky black hair hanging over her shoulder, hazel eyes staring back at him. "Isn't that why we're here right now?" she asked.

"We're here because you paid for a date with me. That date is twenty-four hours in my playroom." He wrapped the tie around her wrist and tied it into a comfortable knot. Easing her arm closer to the iron post, he tied the other half of the silk there in a much tighter configuration.

She did not resist his efforts which was one in a long line of shocks that were hitting him where she was concerned.

"You weren't my type back then," he said when she continued to stare at him.

"Am I your type now?" she asked and slid her hand along his dick again.

"I'm giving you what you paid for," he told her.

"But you're getting something out of this too. I can tell." She looked down at her hand, at the way her fingers were wrapped around his length, her complexion a little lighter than his own. The milky white dot of his arousal leaked from his tip to slide over her finger.

"Tell me I'm wrong." She slowly removed her hand from him, bringing it up to her mouth where her tongue snaked out to lick the drop of his arousal from her skin.

Cris had a knack for going one step too far on many occasions. Her mother had warned her about it after she'd taken her anger at her oldest brother to a costly level by throwing red paint on his black dirt bike because he'd blacked-out the faces of everyone on her Jagged Edge poster.

Talking to Dylan when he obviously did not want to talk was most likely a problem. From what she knew of the BDSM lifestyle the dominant was always in control. She should have been doing whatever he instructed her to do. At least, that's how she thought it worked. But Cris was no submissive. There wasn't a submissive bone in her body, much to her mother's consternation. Without any desire to submit, her old fashioned southern mother was certain her only daughter would never make a good wife. Cris loved her mother but her antiquated beliefs were not shared.

But back to the matter at hand. Or rather, back to Dylan's hand which was now gripping her right tit while his mouth was glued to her left one. He'd watched her licking his essence off her hand and then he'd moved, pushing her back onto the bed, one arm extended by the tie to the post, the other he'd held to the mattress. But that was only for the first few moments as he stared down at her with a gaze so pensive she actually lost her breath.

He slid his fingers slowly down her arm at that point, until his hand was cupping her breast and then he closed his eyes. She'd thought with pleasure from touching her, but he shook his head. Almost like he was telling her no, she had it all wrong. Cris had been afraid that would be the outcome of her returning to D.C. in the first place. So far, nothing, until this very moment had gone as she'd planned on this trip.

Nothing, except the pleasure she'd known she would find under his touch.

The sound of him cursing yanked Cris out of the pleasure haze and she opened her eyes to see him moving away from her. He grabbed the white box she'd seen him take out of the cabinet and opened it. A condom packet and a tube of lube were now in his hand. He pushed the box off the bed and moved between her spread legs.

"This is not the way it goes," he said tersely.

"I'm allergic remember," she began saying after he'd ripped the condom packet, pulled it out and began sliding it down his length.

He finished and looked down at her with his hands still on his thickness. "I didn't need your first or second reminders. I remembered your allergy from the day you first learned of it."

Her mouth formed an "o" but no sound followed. She probably had told him about the allergy when she originally found out in her sophomore year at Howard. She'd initially thought she had an STD and was definitely planning to kill her boyfriend if that turned out to be the case. But why would Dylan have remembered that, of all things, about her?

The sight of him touching himself...no, the mere sight of Dylan naked on a bed between her legs was taking her breath away. She had thought about this moment, but she'd never really believed it would happen. Nine years ago they were the best of friends. They'd gone through a lot together and had held each other down through some pretty trying events as they grew into the adults they were meant to be. But this, sex, was never supposed to happen between them. They'd never discussed taking their friendship to this level, yet, anticipation was running rampant through her body. Arousal filled her so completely she could barely whisper her next words, "You won't need any lube."

He set the tube aside and touched a palm to her inner thigh, pressing it back. It felt as if she were opening for him, especially when he did the same with her other thigh. Cris had never been modest, but Dylan's open perusal of her made her heart beat faster. Up to this point she'd been operating on a mixture of curiosity and bravado. Now that she was certain he was only seconds away from plunging deep inside of her, she could barely keep her limbs from shaking.

She was really getting ready to have sex with Dylan. In his playroom. With one arm tied to the bed post.

He paused for a moment, just staring down at her and Cris wondered if anyone had ever come just from a man's intense gaze. She wiggled her toes and pulled her bottom lip between her teeth while she waited for him to make the next move. But he didn't do anything except stare. Her body hummed with arousal, her nipples were so hard and her breasts so full she wanted to moan with the building arousal and anticipation. Instead, she moved her free hand to cup her breast. Maybe Dylan needed more stimulation.

"I'm ready, Dylan," she whispered. "I'm ready for you."

His gaze shifted to meet hers and Cris gasped at the raw passion she saw in his eyes. Dylan's normally deep brown eyes had grown darker until they almost looked black. A muscle twitched in his jaw and when he lowered his face to hers she parted her lips in anticipation of a kiss she knew would drive them both over the edge. But Dylan stopped short just inches from her lips. He closed his eyes and touched his forehead to hers.

"One night." His voice was a hoarse whisper. "One damn night."

He yanked away from her in the next instant and found the second silk tie. Her other arm was tied to the opposite bedpost in seconds and then Dylan was between her legs once more. He touched a finger gently to the swollen lips of her vagina and Cris gasped again. She'd been confused by him not kissing her and then a bit hurt by his strained words, but now he was touching her and she was melting beneath the heat of desire.

Up and down he stroked her until her arousal soaked not

only her lips, but the one finger he used in such a tantalizing manner. Her thighs began to shake as she arched her back and closed her eyes. In her mind she begged him to make her come, to end this delicious torture that was driving her mad. But she did not speak the words. She could not. Whatever his process, however this impromptu evening needed to play out, Cris was going to let it. She believed wholeheartedly in fate and things that were meant to be. Hadn't that really been the reason she came back to D.C., to find out if she and Dylan were meant to be more than just friends?

Well, she was about to find out.

The thick head of his dick pressed against her entrance and Cris's eyes shot open. He was over her, staring down at her while his body demanded entrance. Cris relaxed her hips and attempted to open her legs wider.

"Keep still," he said through clenched teeth. "Don't move until I tell you."

She froze at his words. Well, froze was not the right word. Cris had never felt more on fire by a man. How it seemed that by doing less than any other guy had ever done to her, Dylan stoked an intense blaze of passion, she had no idea. But it was the truth. This was the most minimal amount of foreplay she'd ever experienced and yet it had effectively made her hotter than ever and more than ready to be fucked.

However, she wasn't going to move. She was going to do exactly as he said because she had a feeling that it was leading to one amazing orgasm. Or two, or three. They had twenty-four hours after all.

Dylan moved over her, pushing his rigid length deeper inside her. It was a good thing she was so wet because he was thick and hard and she could feel her body stretching to accommodate him. Their gazes remained locked as he moved and she welcomed him, until he was fully ensconced inside. Cris moved her arms and remembered they were tied to the bed. She wanted to wrap her arms around his neck and pull him close to her. She wanted to hold him to her so their connection could not be broken. But she could not.

Dylan had flattened his palms on the bed, one on each side of her face, holding the top half of his body away from hers. He began pumping into her, slowly at first and then with a more upbeat rhythm. She lifted her legs and clasped her ankles around his waist, circling her hips in tune with his.

"I told you not to move," he said through gritted teeth.

Cris didn't stop. It felt too good. And neither did Dylan. That muscle in his jaw continued to twitch until Cris thought he may actually be hurting himself. But that thought quickly vanished when his thrusts quickened. Her breath came in heavy pants as she kept up with his pace, loving the feel of him filling her and rubbing along every sensitive nerve ending she possessed. His gaze dropped to her breasts that were now bobbing with the motion of their bodies, but quickly returned to her face. He looked as if he were straining hard to hold something back. She wanted him to let whatever it was out, but without her hands she didn't know how.

"I knew it would be like this," she said as the pleasure intensified and her thighs began to tremble around him. "I always knew."

Dylan didn't speak, but his breaths were coming faster, the muscles in his bare arms bulging as he continued to move over her.

"Did you know, Dylan? Did you ever wonder about us?" she asked partly because the words were now just falling from her lips and because it was something she'd always wondered.

He did not answer. But his strained silence gave way to a deep moan and then a guttural curse. Cris was so wet the sound of him slipping in and out of her echoed in the room. Hadn't she told him no lube would be required? Words were lost in her mind as Dylan eased her legs from around him, holding one ankle in each of his hands. He was on his knees now with her legs spread into a wide V as he pumped mercilessly into her.

Cris moaned. She gasped and pulled at the restraints holding her arms. He'd left plenty of slack between the tie and the bedpost so she was able to twist her wrists and grab hold of the material, squeezing with the intense build of her release. One minute Dylan was deep and the next he was pulled out almost to the tip. On and on this continued for what seemed like forever and at the same time passed too quickly. Her body tensed, and her thighs shook as her release ripped free. She bit down on her lip to the point she was certain to draw blood. Her eyes closed of their own volition and only by sheer stubbornness did she hold onto the scream that desperately wanted to rip free.

Dylan was right behind her. His body tensing on that last thrust so that he was completely embedded inside her as his release poured into the condom. His hands tightened around her ankles and she could hear his loud moan followed by a soft curse. Moments later when they were both still, except for the rapid beating of their hearts, Dylan slipped out of her. He eased her legs down onto the bed. Cris opened her eyes just in time to see him move off the bed to the side where he untied her first wrist. Going to the other side he did the same with the second one. And then he was gone. He walked past the bed and continued going until she heard the soft click of a door.

"Well, damn," Cris whispered. If this is what she had to look forward to for the next twenty-three hours, she was thinking that forfeiting her savings may have actually been worth it.

But then she heard the door open again. He was coming back. For round two? So soon? Well, this time she definitely did not want her hands tied. She wanted to touch him and...Cris's thoughts were cut short as she came up to rest on her elbows and saw Dylan, still naked standing beside the bed.

"This was a mistake. I'm giving you a full refund." His curt words were followed by a stack of cash being tossed on the bed.

Cris was so stunned by the sight of the bills fanning out over the rumbled sheet that she barely noticed the naked guy walking away, again.

3

*H*e was an idiot.

A rude and foolish idiot who was now hiding in his bathroom like a scared child.

Dylan rested his palms on the counter around the sink. He dropped his head and sighed deeply.

What the fuck are you doing?

How many times had he asked that question only to repeatedly come up with no answer?

This was never supposed to happen. Ever!

He and Cris were only ever meant to be friends. Dylan had accepted that a long time ago. He'd accepted a lot of things because he'd had no other choice. Life wasn't meant to give everybody exactly what they wanted, when they wanted it. Those were not the rules.

Speaking of rules, he'd broken so many of them tonight.

First and foremost, there'd been too much talking and touching. Cris was always the talker of their duo. She always had questions or commentary about everything from the weather to writing letters to congressman. In fact, she was part of the reason Dylan had chosen his professional path. Cris was fearless and tenacious. She was smart and intriguing and could light up any room she walked into. The latter usually led to every guy in that room flocking to her like bees to honey. Every guy except Dylan.

He lifted his head and looked into the mirror frowning at the eyes staring back at him.

Cris was not for him.

There'd been so many nights he'd recited those words after being with her. What she deserved—a loving relationship with a man who respected and cared for her well-being—was not something he was able to give. Whether by choice or circumstance, it was a simple fact. Dylan was not into romantic connections. He'd been born into a loveless marriage with two people who had professional plans. Those plans never included a child, but when he came along they did the best that they could, carrying him from state to state and sometimes country to country as they continued on with their business. And the moment that was not possible, they'd dumped a seventeen year-old Dylan at a home in Chicago to live with complete strangers for the second half of his senior year in high school.

Which was how Dylan came to be in his current predicament. Mama Peaches meant a lot to him. So when she'd called him with a request, Dylan hadn't been able to tell her no, especially after learning what was at stake. He still remembered that conversation.

"It's about time you answered that phone. I know you keep it glued to your hip so you must have been ignoring me."

Peaches Brighton had spoken the moment Dylan answered the phone at a little after seven one morning three weeks ago.

"Hey, Mama Peaches. No I haven't been ignoring your call. I've just been really busy with a case that's getting ready to go to trial." The moment the words were out Dylan prayed he hadn't just set himself up for a speech. Mama Peaches, as he'd been told to call her the morning his parents dropped him off at her house, was not one for excuses. She believed everyone should always take full responsibility for their actions, whether good or bad.

"You work too hard. But I guess you got that honestly," Mama Peaches continued. "But I've got something to fix that. I need you to clear your calendar for the last weekend in March. Book yourself a flight and come out here to help me save Southlake Park."

Southlake was the area in Chicago where Mama Peaches lived and Dylan had stayed for six months. It was a small tight-knit community situated along Lake Michigan.

"We need to raise some money to help rebuild the neighborhood. Now that my Harold's gone, I gotta get this done before the good Lord calls me home too. Now, we've got some support from some of the small business owners that have managed to stay in business, but we gotta get more. That's where you come in. I want you to be part of the Bachelor Auction. A fine looking gentleman like you can bring in some big bucks."

For a moment Dylan had thought he was dreaming. Was Mama Peaches really asking him to sell himself so that she could raise money to rebuild a failing black community? The latter was the only reason Dylan continued entertaining the conversation. That and the fact that hanging up on Mama Peaches was definitely not an option.

"How about I just make a donation," he'd suggested.

"How about you stop playing with my nerves and do what I told you to do. You are not too old and educated to get a whop on the head. Probably what you need to get yourself together anyway." Mama Peaches was never one to mince words.

"Who's running this project besides you, Mama Peaches? Have you contacted your congressman about the neighborhood and its contributions to the community? There has to be a way to get some state help in keeping Southlake Park alive." Dylan was not going to deny how much he'd learned during his time in Southlake or how much he'd seen the black business owners and community leaders sacrificing to make the best environment possible for the children growing up there.

"Geraldine's helping me but I don't know about no politics and stuff. I just know we have to stand up and fight for what's ours because nobody else gives a damn. So you get on back here and plan to look sharp and pull in a lot of money for us. Who knows, you may end up finding someone you can spend more time with. Cause that work ain't 'gon keep you warm at night."

That conversation had been short and sweet and an hour later Dylan had made his flight and hotel reservations. He was going back to Chicago. He was also going to do some investigating into the Southlake Community Restoration Project.

Now, however, he needed to figure how something that had started out with his best intentions had gone so horribly wrong. He rubbed a hand over his face and recalled more recent memories. Like the night he sat at The Corporation watching

Cris, watch him get a hand job. Dylan shook his head. He turned on the water and cupped his hands beneath the flow, bringing them up to douse his face in the cool liquid. He did not want to relive that moment at The Corporation. Not the feel of that woman's hand on his dick, or the look of pure unadulterated arousal on Cris's face as he came.

Dylan shut off the water, pushing the faucet with much more force than was necessary. He reached for a towel and pressed it to his face. Inhaling deeply and then releasing the breath slowly he cursed and tossed the towel down onto the counter. What the hell was he going to do now that he'd had sex with the one woman he'd sworn to never touch?

Cris pressed her arms into her jacket and pulled it onto her back with jerky motions. She grabbed her purse that she didn't even recall setting on the table with the towels and headed to the door. When her hand touched the knob she paused. Her twenty-four hours wasn't up, but he'd refunded her money, so it didn't really matter what the agreement was. She turned back, looking at the money on the bed. She hadn't touched it, not to count it and not to curse Dylan any more than she already had.

For someone without all the details it would appear she'd just been paid for her services. Cris knew that wasn't what the money was for, but she couldn't help feeling irritated anyway.

How dare he toss money on the bed and walk away as if dismissing her. And why had she readily foregone any clean-up time in the bathroom and dressed so hastily she'd forgotten to put on her bra? It was now stuffed into the front pocket of her jeans. Leaving was exactly what he wanted her to do. But staying would be mortifying.

She opened the door and walked out before she thought to do otherwise. Slamming it closed behind her was only momentarily rewarding. Pulling her phone out of her purse she called for an Uber as she entered the elevator and tried like hell to convince herself this wasn't as bad as she thought.

But it was.

And two hours later when Cris stepped out of a steaming hot bath and picked up her vibrating phone, she knew that without a doubt.

Meet me at Tony's tomorrow at 5.

The text message seemed like a simple request, but Cris should have remembered, there was never anything simple about her life.

"Hello?"

Cris barely opened her eyes as she grabbed the phone from the table beside the bed and swiped a finger over its screen.

"Well, hello. Nice of you to answer this time. I thought I was going to have to get on a plane and fly up there just to speak to my child."

There was a frosty tone to Celestine Palmer's voice. It was joined by the judgmental silence that always followed her words. Cris fell back onto the pillows dropping an arm over her eyes and cursing herself for not looking at the phone screen to see who was calling before answering. Not that she would have continued to ignore her mother for too long, but she definitely wasn't in the mood to speak to her today.

"Hey, Mama."

"Don't "hey" me. I've been calling you for the past two days. Your voice mailbox is full. That's not professional, you know. What if it were an emergency? You cannot just ignore my calls, Cristine. It's rude and disrespectful."

"I was traveling," Cris said knowing the excuse would not be accepted.

"Traveling? Again? When do you plan to settle yourself down and act like an adult? You left New York a couple weeks ago. Then you were in D.C. Where are you now? And what traveling are you doing if you've quit your job?"

Cris didn't know what time it was but she was betting that it was too early to be questioned with this much intensity. She pulled the phone away from her ear and lifted her arm slightly so she could peek at the screen. Seven-thirty-five. Who in the world called a person to yell at them at seven-thirty-five in the morning? Celestine Palmer, that's who.

"I'm back in D.C., Mama. I'll be here for a while." At least that was Cris's initial plan. She had a couple of interviews lined up at firms and was going to look for apartments this week. The quick jaunt to Chicago caused her to cancel an appointment to look at one apartment building. She would call them back today to see if she could reschedule.

"Why D.C.? You know you belong here in Charleston. Your father has an office waiting for you at the company. He's been holding that position since the day you graduated from law school."

"I'm not coming to work for Daddy." Cris had repeated

those words at least five times a year since she graduated from law school.

Jeremiah Palmer owned Goldpike Insurance Company, one of the largest home, auto and life insurance companies on the east coast. Each of his three sons had followed in Jeremiah's footsteps attending Clemson University and going to work at the insurance company after their graduation. Cris was the only one to break the mold. Her parents had not taken kindly to that.

"You're being stubborn and for no good reason. You have no business running around from state to state on your own. Not when you can come back home where you'll be safe."

"I'm not unsafe, Mama. Besides that, I'm an adult. I can take care of myself wherever I live."

"But if you came home I could keep an eye on you. And don't argue with me about that, I'm your mother and it's my job to take care of you."

Not for my entire life. Cris wisely did not speak those words. Instead she tried to take slow and steadying breaths. It was the only way to survive conversations with her mother.

"Anyway, I'm calling for another reason. You know your father's sixtieth birthday is coming up and I'm planning a big celebration. I want to make sure you're going to be here. Daniel Sanderson is coming. His parents own that department store franchise and Daniel was responsible for their international expansion."

And now she was matchmaking. Cris resisted the urge to groan and hang up the phone.

"Of course I'll be there for Daddy's party. And yes, I remember Daniel. But I'm not looking for a husband."

This was something else Cris had to tell her mother numerous times a year. Actually, this conversation had begun the day after Cris graduated from high school. Because Celestine married Jeremiah when she was seventeen years old, she thought it made perfect sense for Cris to come right out of school, find herself a good husband and settle down to have a family. Cris wasn't totally adverse to the idea of building a family, she just had a professional plan she wanted to see to fruition first.

"Nonsense, you'll be thirty years old next year. If you think your body is going to wait forever to make babies, you're mistaken. Things dry up and stop working in no time at all for women. You don't have any more time to waste. Now, Daniel is a nice boy. He's handsome and has a house down here. I think his mother said he also bought a vacation home on some island, you know how Earlene likes to brag about her boy. So you should get here a week before the party so we'll have time to shop for a dress."

Cris rolled over, pulling the pillow over her head while her mother continued to talk. There was really no need for her to speak at the moment because Celestine wasn't going to hear a word she said. Once her mother started with a plan she was like a primly dressed bulldozer.

4

*D*ylan sighed heavily when the door to his office finally closed. It was almost four-thirty and this was the first time today he'd been alone. He had meetings with two clients this morning and this afternoon he'd met with the three associates in his group. As one of the youngest partners at Loman Regent, Dylan supervised the firm's lobbying division. He was currently involved in training the three associates to not only serve as registered District of Columbia lobbyists, but to also offer their clients the assurance that other lobbyists they selected were also complying with all registration and reporting requirements.

In addition to his full workload, Dylan had been making calls to a few businesses in Chicago in an effort to get a better handle on what was going on in the Southlake area. He was currently waiting for a call back from the owner of one of the few black-owned banks in the Chicago area. In his calls Dylan had uncovered a rent control issue that local business owners and residents had been dealing with for far too long. He wanted to do something about it sooner rather than later.

Dylan had just sat back in his chair, letting his head rest on the soft leather and closed his eyes when there was a quick knock on his door. He lifted his head and was saying "come in" as his assistant, Gwen, was entering the office.

"Leiland wants to set up a conference call at four-thirty. I told him you had an out-of-the-office meeting on your schedule, but that I would check to confirm your unavailability. So, I'm confirming, you're not available, because you skipped lunch. You should leave now, get an early dinner, catch a movie, take a walk, do something besides sit up in this office and work."

Gwen Harris was a fifty-four year old black woman who didn't look as if she was a day over twenty-nine. Today she wore a dark green dress with a black jacket and flat black shoes. Her hair was neatly styled in big curls that circled her face, while her gold-rimmed glasses sat atop high cheekbones on mocha-hued skin. She'd been his assistant for the past eight years he'd been with the firm but tended to act more like a mother hen than a paid employee. After spending six months with Mama Peaches, Dylan was able to stand a little mothering. He hardly ever wondered why his biological mother had never been able to do what had come so easily to these other two women.

"You're right, I am unavailable. Leiland wants to talk about the Channing Group and their push for laws lowering the age of gun permit applicants."

Gwen shook her head as she placed a folder on top of Dylan's inbox and removed the letters he'd signed from the outbox beneath it.

"And that's the stupidest thing I've ever heard. With all

these mass shootings going on around the world, that's the last thing anybody should be thinking about. Hell, I didn't know if I was coming or going when I was eighteen, no way I would have known how to handle a gun responsibly."

"I agree. I'm starting to think that twenty-one might be too young as well, but we definitely weren't hired to lower the minimum age. I'd really prefer he work with Mike Hall or Pete Bivins on that."

"Well, you know why he wants you, because you're the best in this group. Mike and Pete may have seniority but you bring in more high-paying clients and you're better at keeping existing clients satisfied. Plus, he likes how you still remain involved in all the bar activities and you're not out here creating a bad reputation for yourself like most of the young lobbyists and politicians around town."

Dylan loosened his tie as Gwen talked. She was his biggest champion in the firm and likewise when it was review time, Dylan had always given Gwen the highest praise. She was his right and left hand at work and he readily acknowledged that he could not do his job half as well without her. As for the reputations she just mentioned, Dylan had made a point of keeping his tarnish-free. Leiland Regent's grandfather had built this firm with his best friend Kreiger Loman. Today the firm was forty-five years old with seven locations around the world. They prided themselves on an impeccable professional relationship and frowned greatly upon any employees who did not do the same. As the only black partner in the D.C. office, Dylan knew he had to walk the straight and narrow at every point in his life. Which is why his membership at The Corporation was under a different name and he never drove his car to the elite sex club, but always used the club's private car service.

That thought had him silently cursing himself again for not making sure Cris made it safely back to her hotel last night. When he'd come out of the bathroom she'd been gone, which was what he expected at the time. It was only later, when he was back at his apartment that he realized how much of an idiot he'd been.

"I'm going to take your advice, Gwen," Dylan said. He leaned forward and logged out of his computer and then stood from his chair.

"You're getting dinner and a movie? How about you find yourself a nice young lady to go with you? I don't know when the last time I heard you say you were going on a date."

Dylan didn't know either. What he did find odd was that Gwen was saying exactly what Mama Peaches had said on the voice message she'd left for him earlier this afternoon. She'd wanted to know how his date had gone last night, telling him that she'd requested all her Gents—that's what she'd called each of the boys she'd either fostered or babysat as a reminder to them to always be gentlemen—participate in the hopes that they could each find a really nice woman to settle down with. So her bachelor auction to save the neighborhood had also been an elaborate matchmaking scheme. Well, Dylan was in no hurry to return Mama Peaches' call and tell her how horribly wrong his date had gone.

"No date. Just going to grab some dinner. I have two new client files to familiarize myself with before I represent them to the D.C. Council next month." Dylan picked up those client files and slipped them into his soft leather briefcase.

"Well, at least go to a nice restaurant and sit down. Order a three course meal and a glass of wine. Relax a little," she told him as she walked toward the door. "You only get one life to live, Dylan. You should try really living it for a change."

While Gwen kept walking out of his office, Dylan had paused. Cris used to wear a white shirt with YOLO in bright pink letters across her breasts. When she'd caught him staring at the letters one day she'd quickly said, "You only live once, Dylan," while pointing at each letter. She'd thought she had to explain what the abbreviation meant, but really Dylan had been enjoying the way the tight white material hugged her breasts and admired those letters for the way they seemed to wrap around the heavy mounds as well.

Now, he shook his head with the thought. He'd finally seen those breasts bare. He'd had them in his hands and in his mouth. If he closed his eyes right now he could recall the sight of her puckered pinkish nipples. His dick jumped and Dylan clenched his teeth. This was going to happen every time he thought about Cris now. There would be no more memories of their friendship or the good times they'd had as just friends, all that would remain in his mind was how good she'd felt and tasted and how badly he wanted to feel and taste her again.

"You're right," he said finally. "I'm going to get some dinner and head home."

He closed his bag and looked up just in time to see Gwen staring warily at him.

"I'm going to a restaurant and I'll sit there and enjoy my meal."

Gwen nodded and gave him a knowing smile. Dylan could admit that the woman was right more than she was wrong.

"Good. I'll see you in the morning."

"Goodnight." Dylan grabbed his cell phone from his desk charger and walked out of his office.

Half an hour later he'd removed his tie and suit jacket. He walked into Tony's Bar and Grille wearing a brown leather jacket and pushing his cell phone into his pocket.

"Hey Dylan. Long time no see, man."

Dylan smiled and accepted the handshake and half hug from Frank "Fisher" Baines, the manager of the restaurant. "Yeah, good to see you too."

"And you're lucky 'cause your favorite booth in the back just became available."

"Ah, well, maybe I could just sit at the bar," Dylan replied.

Fisher had stepped behind a dark wood pedestal where a hostess was holding a tablet. He looked down at it and then up to Dylan after he spoke.

Fisher tilted his head and frowned. "What's going on with you two?"

"Excuse me?"

"Cris is here and she didn't want to sit at your booth either."

Dylan immediately looked around the dining room area. "What do you mean Cris is here?"

Fisher came back to stand at Dylan's side. He put a hand on Dylan's shoulder and turned him slightly to the left. "She's right over there. Came in about ten minutes ago and specifically said she did not want your booth."

Dylan heard Fisher talking but he wasn't listening to the words he was saying. He was too busy staring at not just Cris at a table, but at the man sitting across from her.

"Sonofa—"

"Hey man, I was just kidding. If this is really a sticky situation, I can sit you down at the back end of the bar. You won't see them and they won't see you. I just thought considering your history together that you and Cris would have been married with kids by now."

Dylan turned his head quickly to stare at Fisher. Why would he have thought he and Cris would be married? They'd come here to eat a lot during their undergrad years, but that's all they'd ever done was eat. There were no PDAs or even hand holding for that matter, because they weren't a couple. They were just friends.

"Nah, it's cool," Dylan replied. "I'll take the booth."

"Whatever you say, boss."

Fisher chatted from the time they left the hostess area until the moment Dylan slipped into the booth and Fisher handed him a menu.

Dylan had only been half listening to Fisher as he'd talked to him and giving what answers he thought were correct. Sitting down now he looked at the menu and frowned. "Come on, Fisher. You know I don't need this."

Fisher grinned, his angular face sporting a jovial expression as usual. "We've added some new stuff since the last time you were here. Just because you're a bigshot lawyer now, don't mean you're the only one who can move it on up."

Dylan chuckled as Fisher broke into his rendition of the George Jefferson dance.

"Bacon double cheeseburger, lettuce tomatoes, mayo and fries," Dylan repeated what he always ordered and did not take the menu.

"We have sweet potato fries now, or you could try the glazed asparagus, it's delicious." Fisher tucked the menu under his arm and spoke as if he'd just offered Dylan something as expensive as caviar but tasted as good a BBQ ribs.

Dylan was not tempted.

"I'll stick with the fries. And a chocolate milkshake with shavings."

Fisher stopped grinning at that point and just stared at Dylan before finally nodding.

"I'll put your order in."

"Thanks, man. It is really good to see you," Dylan replied sincerely. It had been a very long time since Dylan had done anything that reminded him of his grad school years.

"Yeah, same here," Fisher said with another nod and smile before leaving Dylan alone.

It wasn't until Fisher walked away that Dylan realized his mistake. He always had a root beer soda with his meal. Cris used to order the milkshake with extra chocolate shavings on top. He pressed the palms of his hands against his eyes and shook his head.

This was not going to end well. He'd known it the moment he'd seen her at The Corporation. Cris was back in D.C. They weren't college kids anymore. She was in a sex club, on his turf. And then, she was in his playroom, on his bed. Now she was in his head and dammit she was sitting in their place with him!

Dylan was slipping out of the booth before he could think better of what he was about to do.

5

"*H*ello, Garrett. Cris you didn't tell me you were seeing Garrett while you were in town."

Cris looked at Dylan standing beside the table and wondered what higher deity she'd pissed off to have such poor luck. How was it that she'd come back to town, finally slept with her best friend, was having dinner with her ex-boyfriend, and was now being confronted by her best friend as if she were caught cheating on him?

"Hey, Dylan." Her voice sounded a lot steadier than she actually felt.

Her heart was thumping in her chest and she was looking from Dylan to Garrett and back to Dylan again, just like she was a cheating girlfriend. It was ridiculous!

Garrett stood and extended his hand to Dylan.

"Good to see you, man. It's been way too long," he said to Dylan with a genuine smile.

Garrett Mason was just an inch or two shorter than Dylan. He had a broader frame than Dylan's toned slim stature and a lighter, tawny brown complexion. While Garrett looked nice in his dark jeans, beige button front shirt and russet colored sports coat, Dylan gave an immediate air of black power and dominance in his navy blue suit, pale blue striped shirt and intense glare. Even without the tie Dylan exerted professionalism and control. His handshake with Garrett was strong, succinct and telling as Dylan had immediately positioned himself to stand closer to Cris, so that he was now physically blocking Garrett from her. As if his appearance alone wasn't enough of which would have quickly been called a cock-block when they were younger.

"It has been a while," Dylan stated evenly before releasing Garrett's hand.

Garrett returned to his seat, his smile a bit more triumphant than Cris thought it should have been.

"I just found out she was here the night before last when I ran into Tisha at a networking event. She said she'd had lunch with Cris the day she came back and they'd talked about apartments and firms that were hiring." Garrett had just given Dylan more information than Cris figured he wanted to hear.

Or at least that's what Cris had assumed. Dylan, however, looked pretty intrigued by Garrett's words.

"Cris knows I'm always looking out for her so if staying in town is her goal, then I'll definitely take care of her."

By tossing cash at her and walking out? That was an odd way of taking care of someone.

"Well, you know I've got a little clout in this town as well, D," Garrett said. Now, the same 'ole ego tug of war these former roommates had years ago was back and Cris twisted the napkin she was holding.

"I've already given her leads on a few defense firms that will snap her up in a hurry. You know there are several firms trying to up their diversity game by bringing in more young black lawyers."

Garrett was a transactional attorney in a large firm. During the fifteen minutes they'd had to chat before Dylan appeared, Cris had also learned that Garrett was very active in the Young Lawyers division of the local bar, as well as a few reputable networking groups for young black professionals, many of which had gone to undergrad with them. Despite their past, Cris had actually been thinking that agreeing to dinner with Garrett had turned out to be a good idea. If she were planning to put down roots in D.C., she definitely wanted to be a part of the professional scene with people who looked like her.

"She shouldn't limit herself to firms only looking to meet their diversity quota. She can do better than that," was Dylan's clipped response.

"I'm keeping my options open," Cris interjected.

This had the potential to get ugly very quickly.

While Garrett was under the impression that he and Dylan were doing their normal back and forth and that he had the upper hand since he and Cris had dated for almost two years, Cris knew the truth. And so did Dylan.

Dylan knew about everything that had gone down between her and Garrett, every very private and humiliating thing. Garrett, of course knew those same things, but he'd had no idea how Cris had felt back then, and she was certain he didn't know now, or he'd never have invited her to dinner. But she'd been willing to put the past behind her and have a mature meal with the guy. Dylan, on the other hand, clearly did not think that was such a good idea.

"We have to get in where we fit in, man. We all can't have our daddy walk us into the biggest lobbying firm in D.C. and drop a partnership in our lap."

And there it was, the proverbial gauntlet being tossed down. Dylan had never been one to walk away from a challenge, especially not with a guy that Cris had to stop him from pummeling years ago.

"Your appetizers are here!" Foster appeared just in time with a waitress carrying a tray right behind him.

"Man it's good to see y'all again after so long," Foster continued, easily stepping into the space between where Dylan still stood close to Cris and where Garrett was sitting, gazing superiorly at Dylan.

"Dylan you want your food brought over here? We can just pull up another chair because it'll be out in a few minutes." Foster looked at Dylan.

Cris didn't have to shift her gaze to him. She could feel the tension radiating from his body. If she released the weird hold she now had on the napkin and extended her hand upward just a bit, she would touch Dylan's hand. Without looking she knew it was fisted at his side because he was barely restraining himself from saying something else to Garrett. Something that Cris knew wasn't going to lead to a smile and more cordial conversation. Foster knew that too.

"No," Dylan finally replied. "I'm going back to my table. Cris, I'll talk to you later."

He did not say another word to Garrett, nor did he spare

Cris a glance before leaving. Foster shrugged and touched Cris's shoulder before leaving the waitress to deliver their food.

"That guy's still full of himself," Garrett said as he quickly began to munch on his cheesesteak egg rolls.

Cris had ordered French onion soup as her appetizer, but she really wasn't in the mood for it now. She'd perused the menu searching for anything other than what she always ordered when she'd come here with Dylan. She wondered what Dylan had ordered.

"Dylan's not a bad guy." She heard the words and hated that her first instinct was to defend him, even though the way Dylan had come over here had been rude and dismissive. And after last night he didn't deserve her defense. Actually, she should have been going over to his table and giving him a few select words for the way he'd treated her.

"He's a pompous ass, just like always. Remember I told you he never liked studying with any of the guys in the house. He didn't do movie nights with us or even the parties. Each time we had a party, he would contribute his fair share to the food and the booze but then he'd disappear like we weren't good enough for his time." Garrett was shaking his head as he chewed. "And then he goes off to law school and one year later while we're all trying to get internships with the local judges or even at a small firm, he nabs a top paying internship at Loman Regent. They hired him as an associate months before he even took the bar. Lucky bastard! Or should I say privileged bastard."

Cris was glad Garrett stuffed another chunk of egg roll into his mouth. She didn't like hearing him speak negatively about Dylan. Even though most of what he'd said was true. Dylan hadn't liked hanging with any of the four guys he'd shared the house with, but not because he thought he was better than them. No, that wasn't it at all. Dylan was an only child and he'd traveled all over the world during his childhood because his father, Hanson, was an international lawyer. His mother, Demetria, also had a law degree but focused more on legal writing than litigating and had created a mobile law firm hiring attorneys across the world to freelance their writing services for global corporations as well as local business. Now, Hanson was a senator. He and his wife had settled here in D.C. one year after Dylan finished grad school. Cris recalled him dreading that possibility every moment of his father's campaign that kicked off the same week as homecoming of their senior year.

"He graduated tops in our class," she said, even though she'd sworn she would only defend Dylan in her mind. "He repeated that in law school and always had an interest in public causes. I think lobbying was a natural fit for him."

Garrett used a napkin to wipe his mouth. He had grown into a handsome man, with his round face and dark wavy hair. His low cut and very neatly trimmed beard gave him a mature look, but his brown eyes still held the hint of laughter that had first drawn her to him.

"I'm not going to spend out first night together in what... eight or nine years years...talking about Dylan James. He can stay right in his penthouse apartment, driving his slick Jaguar and wearing five hundred dollar suits. I'm just happy to be sitting across from you, the prettiest girl on the east coast." Garrett smiled. He set the napkin on the table and reached over to touch her hand.

She'd meant to pick up her spoon and begin eating her

soup, but her hand had remained still on the table. Now, it was being folded into Garrett's and a tingle of discomfort settled in the pit of Cris's stomach.

"I'm sure you've found another "prettiest girl on the east coast" by now," she said, while slightly easing her hand away from his.

Dinner with Garrett was one thing. Being touched by Garrett was something totally different.

"Nobody will ever compare to you."

She nodded and managed to pick up the spoon at that point. As far as smooth comebacks go, that was pretty good. She sipped the soup and wished like hell she'd ordered the onion rings like she used to do.

"No. They'll just be better in bed than me," she quipped after swallowing the first spoonful and admitting the best part of the soup was the cheese. "Or a better dancer than me. Or no, more outgoing than me. Which, is really crazy since I was involved in more stuff on campus than you, or any of the three, no four, girls you cheated on me with."

Talking about her past was something else Cris hadn't intended on doing. Although, she wasn't sure what Garrett thought tonight was going to be after the way they'd left things the start of their junior year. By that time, Cris had taken all that she was going to take from Garrett. And the fact that her ex-roommate Tisha, who coincidentally had been the one to tell Cris about Garrett's last dalliance, had not only told Garrett she was back in town, but had also given him her phone number, was something Cris was determined to deal with as well.

"Whoa. We're adults now, Cris. Why do we have to go there?"

He was right. She knew it. But she was still bristling from Dylan's mysterious appearance. Had he known she was going to be there? And if so, how would he have known? And why the hell would he care?

"We have a past, Garrett. Now, I can sit here and share this meal with you and we can talk about all the things going on in our lives right now, but that past isn't going to vanish."

The waitress appeared with their entrees. Cris frowned at the grilled salmon she'd ordered and wondered if it would be rude to ask for a box and get the hell out of here right now.

"We do have a past," Garrett continued when they were once again alone. "I apologized for it back then and if it'll make you feel better, I'll apologize again now. I'm sorry I was a horny idiot. I should have cherished what I had. But that time has passed and I'm hoping we can start again, tonight."

"Start what again?"

Cris needed to be perfectly clear about what Garrett thought this dinner was.

"Our friendship. I'm going to help you get a job, find a place and get settled because that's what friends do. And then, I'm hoping you'll see how much I've changed, how much we've both changed, and then realize that we were always meant to be together."

She took another sip of the soup. It had grown cold and the cheese was no longer as tasty as she'd thought. Cris set the spoon down and picked up her napkin from her lap. She wiped her fingers on the napkin and dabbed it to her lips before setting it on the table beside the salmon.

"Here's the thing. I appreciate the leads you gave me and the gesture of helping me. But I can find my own job and place to live. And as far as how much we've both changed, you're absolutely right. We are two very different people than when we were in grad school. Which is why, I'm going to get up and walk out of here right now. The young Cris that you declared your love to and disrespected every chance you could, is gone. The adult Cris who also graduated tops in grad and law school, has too much going on in her life to entertain your self-centered bullshit again. But thanks, it was nice catching up."

She stood, grabbed her jacket off the back of the chair, her purse and left Garrett sitting there with his mouth gaped open.

6

"*I*nvite me in, Cris."

She crossed her arms over her chest and arched a brow. "What the hell are you doing here? You following me now?"

"Invite me in so we can talk."

"Oh? Now we're going to talk? Last night it was "here, take this money and get the hell out"."

"That's not what I said."

"It's what your actions said."

"I don't want to have this conversation from the hallway."

"Then perhaps you should have called first."

"Cris."

"Dylan."

They stood in silence staring at each other for much longer than Dylan wanted. He could step forward and she would move back. Then he would be inside the room and she wouldn't do anything but close the door behind him and continue her tirade. But he didn't. She had to consent, even to him being in her room just to talk, Dylan waited for her consent.

"Your food is going to get cold," he said after a few moments more.

Her lips tilted upward as she narrowed her eyes. "You're not slick."

She turned and walked away, leaving the door open and him standing there. A silent consent. Dylan was going to go with that.

He stepped inside the room and closed the door behind him, clicking the locks into place. She'd moved across the room to where a large green and white bag with Tony's printed in block red letters sat on top of a table. A cup which he was certain was filled with a chocolate milkshake and chocolate shavings was a short distance from the bag. Closer to the cup was a container with a clear lid, a double cheeseburger with lettuce, grilled onions, extra mustard and pickles and a side order of fresh-cut fries was inside.

Cris dropped down into the chair in front of her food. She picked up a fry and stuffed it into her mouth.

"How did you know where I was?"

Dylan removed his jacket and hung it on the back of the chair on the other side of the table. He eased down slowly into that chair and moved the Tony's bag to the floor because it prevented him from seeing her face.

"Fisher called you a cab while you waited at the far end of the bar for your food," he told her.

She chewed and nodded. "He didn't want Garrett following me outside and causing trouble, but he willingly gives you the name of the hotel where I'm staying. He has no clue."

Dylan glanced out the window that was right beside the table. The hotel was in the Dupont Circle area of the city. A few of the restaurants lined on Connecticut Avenue were in sight, yet Cris had turned up at Tony's on the same night that Dylan had decided to return there. Fate? Karma? Bad luck? A blessing?

Dylan had no idea what this was, but he knew he had to get a handle on it before things got way out of hand.

"Last night was a mistake."

She'd taken a bite of her cheeseburger during his silent contemplation. He watched her chew. Her hair was straight resting on her shoulders in dark strands. The make-up around her eyes was smoky and made her look a little older, more exotic. The raisin colored lipstick she'd been wearing at the restaurant was just about gone now as her mouth slowed its movements and she lifted the napkin to wipe her lips. She picked up her cup, sipped from the straw and then sat back in her chair. Not one of her movements or gestures was practiced or calculated. She was doing exactly as she would do if she were at her home, or his home, wherever she was comfortable. Because that's how they were together, how they'd always been. Totally comfortable, relaxed, at ease, in tune with each other on a level that nobody else had been able to reach.

Like a punch to the gut, Dylan realized how much he'd missed that feeling.

"I paid for a date. I got a partial delivery of what I paid for and a full refund." She shrugged. "I'm sure those types of transactions happen all the time."

"You didn't take the money."

"It was given for a good cause."

"You always give away your body for free?"

"Well, since I'm not a prostitute, I guess that answer is yes. And furthermore, the Southlake Restoration Project is a very good cause. I researched it and am actually interested in seeing if I can do more to help. So, sorry Dylan, your grand gesture is a no go."

He watched her sit up and reach for her burger again. She ate with a gusto that said she was absolutely enjoying every bite. Dylan was glad for her. He'd only managed a couple bites of his burger before he noticed she'd gotten up from her table, at which time he immediately got up to follow her. But a signal from Foster who'd been standing precariously close to both of their tables, said the other man had it under control. Still, Dylan had lost his appetite. His bigger concern had been for what had happened with Garrett and whether or not Cris was alright.

"I know you're not a prostitute, Cris. Don't make it sound like I'm the bad guy in this."

"Aren't you? I mean, I paid for something, I signed your crazy consent form and then you reneged. What's up with that?"

"You weren't supposed to be there. We weren't supposed to do that. None of it should have happened."

"But it did," she snapped back. "We had sex, Dylan. Mighty good sex even if a bit on the freaky side. I accepted some of your terms and was in it for the long haul, but you quit on me."

"I'm trying to save our friendship."

"Oh?" She finished chewing a fry. "I didn't know our friendship was in danger. I mean, unless you're considering the fact that you haven't had a moment to return any of my calls since I've been back in town."

"You haven't called since you left for law school," he stated solemnly.

She stopped chewing. Stopped acting as if eating was her biggest priority now and stopped giving him that I-got-the-upper-hand look.

"I knew where you were but I couldn't see you the way I was used to doing. And that was cool," he told her. At first it had been hard when she was gone. But about three months after she left he reminded himself that this was how life was. People moved on. They went wherever they needed to go to do the things they needed to do to progress in their lives. Hadn't that been what his parents had done, even with him in tow?

"We both had plans for our future. I was going to stay here and go into law where I could help with future legislation without becoming a full-blown politician. And you were going to take the corporate world by storm with your quick analytical mind and no-nonsense demeanor. You were going to be what most feared, a strong and intelligent black woman who understood the law better than most lawyers currently practicing."

She shrugged. "We had big plans."

"And we needed the time and space to see them through. You not only passed the New York bar, but you went on to take Maryland's bar as well and gained a high enough score to waive into D.C.'s without having to take another bar exam. Karpinski, Lee and Cross were lucky to snag you after you'd already received multiple offers."

Cris tilted her head and let her hands fall to her lap as she stared quizzically at him. "You kept tabs on me?"

Dylan lifted his leg to let his ankle rest on his thigh. He propped one elbow up on the arm of the chair. "We had plans. I was following through with mine and wanted to make sure you were doing the same."

Which still equated to keeping tabs on her.

"You did exactly what you said you would do," she said. "Except—"

Dylan knew exactly what she was going to say next. He hadn't wanted to ever talk about this with her, but after last night, he'd known he had no other choice.

"Except what?" Just because he knew what she wanted to talk about, didn't mean he had to make it any easier for either of them.

"When did you become a dominant?" The words rolled from her mouth as easily as if she said them every day.

Dylan was intrigued.

"I'm not a dominant." It was a simple reply, one which he knew would never satisfy her curiosity.

"I didn't think so, at least not in the conventional sense. So what are you? What do you like and why?"

He rubbed a finger over his chin. The goatee was still low cut as he hadn't decided whether or not he liked it enough to keep. Cris hadn't mentioned it at all so he wasn't sure if she liked or disliked it either.

"In sexual relationships, distance works for me. Over the years I've experimented with different activities that allow me to achieve the most pleasure for both myself and my partner, while maintaining the separation that I require."

"Sex is an up close and personal experience, unless you're into cyber or phone sex. So how or why exactly is distance such a big deal to you?"

She would dissect his words with the precision of a trial attorney.

"I just like it that way."

"Did you like it last night?"

"I did."

"Then why did you kick me out?"

"I didn't tell you to leave."

"You gave me a refund, Dylan. Short of saying "get dressed and get going", that's exactly what the money on the bed meant."

He was curious. "Why didn't you take it?"

"Like I said before, it's a good cause. I actually plan on checking back with Mama Peaches and her lively friend Geraldine, whom I met at the auction, in the coming months to see how everything is going."

"You don't know her or that neighborhood."

"But you do," she replied. "I remember you telling me about the six months you stayed there during your senior year in high school. And after seeing the loyalty and devotion from each one of the men that Mama Peaches helped to raise, I figured she's a good woman doing a great work."

Cris was an enigma. For as well as Dylan was sure he knew her, she could still surprise him. Why had she remembered where he'd been before she'd met him in college? And why wasn't she more alarmed or offended about his sexual preference? Hadn't that been one of the main reasons Dylan had kept it a secret, because he wasn't sure how people would think about him if they knew? Not that he was one to care about other people's opinions of him, he just didn't like drama of any kind, and explaining the reasons for his sexual preference was definitely likely to bring some drama into his life.

Cris stood from the chair while his silence stretched on.

"I'm curious," she said as she came around the table and stopped in front of him. "I guess you could say I've been wondering about you, in a sexual way, for a very long time."

Dylan's gaze followed her movements. He watched her slim legs covered in navy blue leggings and the rise and fall of her breasts in the blue and white blouse that barely brushed her upper thighs. She was wearing flat shoes today for an ensemble that should not have been as outrageously sexy as it appeared. At the restaurant her hair had been pulled back to hang in a long straight tail. Now, it was free, falling around her shoulders in an alluring sheet of darkness.

"We used to spend so much time together." She stood about three feet away from him, one leg extended a little in front of the other, her arms folded across her chest.

"I never had a friend like you," Dylan admitted. Even though now he wasn't looking at her as a friend.

"I know." The words came with a slight chuckle and a quick flash of her brilliant smile. "That was so weird. I grew up with brothers so confiding in a guy was the furthest thing from my mind while growing up. But then, I met you."

"And it was different." He could totally relate to that because meeting her had been different for him too. Right from the start. So he shouldn't be so surprised that now he wanted...

but it wasn't supposed to be this way. How many times had he told himself that?

She tilted her head. "So very different," she whispered and then took a step toward him.

Her hands fell to her sides as she took another step, until her knee brushed against his.

"Toward the end of our senior year," she said softly. "That's when I started to wonder if our friendship was something more. We'd both been single for months by that time and when we weren't in class, we were together."

"Because that was safe. If we were together nobody else was trying to be with us. We wanted to remain single, free to pursue our careers and nothing else." That's what they'd told themselves. Dylan had been elated to find someone in such total agreement with the plan he'd come up with for his adult life.

She nodded. "It worked perfectly. Except, I don't think we paid enough attention to how much we were together, how well we worked together, how effortless our togetherness had become."

He knew where she was going with this. The insane thought had dashed through his mind a time or two after she'd left for New York.

"And then we moved on," he said with a finality that was meant to break whatever had started to weave its way around them.

It felt like some unseen gauzy net that had been laid and was now closing around them, pulling them closer together. Inside Dylan felt like squirming. He wanted to break free before it was too late, but then she touched him. She put a hand on his knee and pushed his leg down until his foot touched the floor. In the next instant she stepped between his now spread legs. Dylan could do nothing but remain sitting back in the chair, his hands falling to his thighs.

"I had no idea I was following you to a place like The Corporation. I was on my way into your building when I saw you come out and get into that truck. There were two taxis waiting at the curb and I just hopped in one and told the driver to follow you."

"I didn't see you," he told her. "If I had I would have stopped you."

Cris began to move, until she was on her knees in front of him. "I'm glad you didn't stop me."

Dylan's teeth clenched tightly.

"I will never forget watching her come between your legs and touch you. The look on your face was so stoic as if you were some type of god waiting to be serviced, to be praised and pleasured. I'd never thought of you that way before."

Her palms were flat on his knees now, moving upward past where his hands rested on his thighs and further. His dick was already jumping, had been since the moment she'd stood in front of him. It knew what Dylan's mind continued to deny.

"You don't understand." His words came through clenched teeth. "You would never understand."

"Make me understand, Dylan," she said without hesitation.

Her hand moved over the bulge of his erection before fingers quickly undid the button of his pants and pulled down his zipper.

"Introduce me to the man you've become and the pleasures that you enjoy."

She had no idea what she was asking of him. No. Fucking. Idea.

While he waited for the right words to register in his mind, the ones that would push her back once and for all, she watched him. Her hand was inside his boxers now, wrapped around his length, freeing the now throbbing erection.

"Let me in, Dylan," she said softly before dipping her head and touching the tip of her tongue to the crest of his dick.

Dylan didn't stop her. He didn't say anything, but his gaze darkened as he sat back in the chair. Cris kept her gaze on his as her tongue circled the slit in his dick. Her breasts felt fuller than they ever had before, her nipples tightening and pressing against the soft material of her bra.

She pulled her tongue back and opened her mouth over the head of his cock. His skin was silky smooth and warm as her tongue and lips clamped over him. The quick moan escaped before she could even consider holding it in. But it was far too late for that. Cris was an all-in type of woman. When she made a decision she followed it through to the end. She'd decided she would come back to D.C. to not only find a new job, but also to see if there was something more between her and Dylan. So far, the something more was definitely an option. A delicious one.

Dylan was still silent even though she'd felt his thigh muscles tense as she rested her arms on him to get a better hold of his dick. Both hands were on him now, one wrapped around the base of his cock, while the other slipped further into his boxers to cup his heavy sac. He still did not speak, just as he had not spoken to that woman in the club who had performed the hand job on him.

Cris cleared that thought from her mind. First, because she definitely did not want to think of being in competition with someone else and second, because Dylan touched a hand to her head. He hadn't touched that other woman.

His fingers slipped slowly through the loose strands of her hair, blunt tips rolling over her scalp. Encouraged, Cris dipped her head lower. She relaxed the muscles of her throat and breathed in deeply as she took in more of his length. Touching her lips to his skin, flattening her tongue against the bottom stretch of his cock, she sucked in her cheeks. His fingers tightened around her hair until he was pulling with just enough encouragement to have her easing back, his length slipping slowly out of her mouth.

Cris held onto him, but inhaled deeply with her lips just inches away from his cock. She looked up to see him staring intently at her.

"I asked about you when we were at the club and was given the name you prefer to go by. Then, at the auction, when you were introduced, they used the same name. Why do they call you "The Master"?"

She did not release her hold on him, loving the feel of his warm length throbbing beneath her touch. When he didn't answer right away she dipped her head lower, taking him into her mouth once more. Now she bobbed her head over him, taking him in and out, stroking him with her hand and mouth until she was breathless from the effort.

He buried another hand in her hair, wrapping the strands

around his fingers and this time tugging her back from his cock with more force. When his dick plopped free of her lips and her breath was coming in heaves, Dylan held her head in his hands, tilting it upward so that she could meet his gaze.

"Because I am the master of pleasure," he whispered.

His voice was so deep and thick with desire that her lips quivered, both the ones on her face and the ones between her legs. The lower sensation was followed by a deep throbbing that signaled need, pure unadulterated sexual need.

Dylan continued to push her back. At the same time he came forward in the chair, until his fingers were falling from her hair and they were both coming to a standing position. He stepped to her and took her mouth in a scorching hot kiss complete with tongues, lips, teeth and moans.

"Let me show you," he growled when he finally tore his mouth away from hers.

Cris didn't have time to ask what she was about to be shown, nor did she care. Dylan had lifted her in his arms, cradling her against his chest like she was a child. He walked them across the room to the bed and set her gently on top of the comforter.

That was where the gentleness stopped.

He leaned forward, his mouth moving savagely against hers. Cris had tilted her head back so far to meet the demand of his kiss that she thought the back of her neck would pop. Her lips were wet from him sucking them both deep into his mouth before plunging his tongue back inside for more.

Then he was pulling away from her. Cris heaved out a breath. She was just about to situate herself on the bed, maybe ask him what was about to happen next, or something along those lines, when he reached for her. Dylan slipped his fingers beneath the rim of her leggings. Cris had no idea how, but he grabbed the ban of her thong as well, pulling both down her legs so fast she fell back on the bed from the motion. He had her bare from the waist down in seconds. Her legs were in the air and spread wide moments later. And then his face was there. His lips on her lips, his tongue delving deep into her center pumping the way his dick had last night.

Cris gasped. Her fingers gripped the comforter and her teeth bit into her bottom lip. His mouth moved with one goal only—infinite pleasure. Sliding up her slit to touch the hood of her clit, he licked and circled, sucked and slurped. Down again he was in her deep, milking every drop of her essence before moaning. She wanted to pump into his face, to grab the back of his head and hold him to her until she exploded, but she couldn't.

Dylan had complete control. His fingers were clamped around her ankles, holding her legs out wide and pushing her back until her ass cheeks weren't even touching the bed. His face was buried inside of her, until her thighs quaked and her eyes rolled back in her head.

"What do you feel?" he asked when he moved his mouth slightly, his warm breath brushing over her damp folds.

Cris couldn't talk. Her answer was a moan and a twist of her hips. She wanted to come. No, she needed it like she needed air. Her body felt so tight she was shaking all over. She was so close and he was talking.

Dylan licked her long and slow. She moaned deep and loud.

"Tell me what you feel," he insisted.

"Pleasure!" she yelled. "So much pleasure that if you don't finish this I swear I'll..."

Cris didn't get to finish her sentence because Dylan had gone in for more. This time he licked from her clit to her center and back further until she was squirming in his grasp. Her eyes were closed tight, her fingers pulling the comforter until she was sure it was lifting off the bed. He came back up licking and sucking, the sound of slurping echoing in the room. She was so wet and so primed to be fucked. Would he put his dick inside her at this moment? Or would he continue this sweet torment with his tongue? She had no clue and she really didn't give a damn. All that mattered was the pleasure and her climax.

The latter came seconds later and she moaned his name as he held her shaking legs tightly.

"Take me to The Corporation," Cris asked half an hour later after they'd both had time in the bathroom and were now laying across the bed.

"Why?"

"Because I want to see it through your eyes. I want to do what you like to do there."

"This is not for you, Cris." Dylan told her. He sat up and dropped his head into his hands. Dragging those hands down his face he sighed heavily.

"None of this is what I planned for us. We're really good friends. That means a lot to me."

"Oh please, don't give me that "we're friends and that's all" spiel. We're way beyond that," she told him. "We are adults.

That's it. And if two consenting adults want to have sex or play at a sex club, they're permitted to do so."

"This can't be what you're thinking. I can't give you what you ultimately want."

"Then for now, give me what I need," she insisted.

7

*T*wo days later Cris stood in an empty bedroom staring out of floor-to-ceiling windows at the fading sunlight. It was a chilly Friday and this was the third apartment she'd looked at today. She was tired and hungry and was thinking that it was just like her to feel drawn to one of the most expensive apartment buildings in the city.

The location was excellent, the view was breathtaking and the space was more than she'd even considered. Basically, the place was winning in all areas, except the price. Cris came from a family where money was not an issue. Her father constantly reminded his children of how hard he worked to make sure that his family was provided for. Jeremiah taught his sons the same work ethic and principles of taking care of the family they would one day build, while Celestine taught Cris how to be the perfect wife. Cris wanted to be a professional, amass her own wealth and be the type of wife she chose to be. The type that could go into a courtroom and win a tough case, then come home and ride her husband until they were both screaming from pleasure.

The latter came from the memory of two nights ago when Dylan had spent the night in her hotel room.

Cris hadn't expected him and truth be told, when he'd arrived at her room she'd been irritated beyond measure that he'd followed her and still confused about what had happened in his playroom the night before. Dylan had explained both incidents but that hadn't made her feel better. His presence made her feel more aroused. After years of being this man's friend and holding back any other feelings for him, her attraction to him seemed to shoot out of the gates now.

When they were in the room together the flame was immediately lit and spread like an inferno in no time. Two nights ago had been more of the same. After their first oral tryst and her request to be taken to The Corporation, Dylan had attempted to talk the way they used to.

"Why'd you come back?" he'd asked. "You were doing well at that firm in New York. Your litigation track record had won you a coveted position in the corporate department and you were entering into international negotiations for some of their top clients. You had it made."

Cris had sat in the center of the hotel bed, wearing a night shirt she'd pulled on after washing up, her legs crossed beneath her.

"It was great in New York. From the time they recruited me to the time I got the promotion. I loved the rush of litigating and winning the unwinnable cases. And the accolades from that propelled me to the promotion. I'd begun traveling for clients and was really making a name for myself."

Dylan finished that sentence for her. "A good, solid professional name. Exactly what you always wanted."

He was right, that was what she'd said she always wanted, to be someone other than Jeremiah and Celestine Palmer's daughter. And she'd made it.

"It wasn't enough," she confided. "I had a great apartment, and a Mercedes I never drove because traffic in New York is horrific. It's not great here in D.C. either which is why Uber has definitely been my friend." She'd chuckled.

"But you weren't happy."

"No," she replied. "I wasn't happy. I thought I would be, you know. We talked so many nights about our planned success and how once we got there everything else would fall in place. But it didn't. I waited and waited, but there was still something missing."

"Something you think you'll find in D.C.?"

She'd shrugged. "I don't know. But I came back here because it was the last place I was happiest. I wanted that feeling again. The energy and the possibility. The comfort and the acceptance."

"It wasn't the same after you left," he admitted.

"Then why didn't you answer when I did finally call you?"

"I'd started my internship by then and only wanted the best for you. I wanted you to soar into your destiny. Remember you used to say that all the time." He'd laughed at the memory and Cris joined him.

"When you finally get your wings under you and begin to fly, you also learn to maneuver your direction. I can be a successful attorney anywhere. I needed to go where my heart and soul could be fulfilled on another level," she said.

"And that's here?"

She'd nodded. "I think so."

His immediate silence afterward meant he didn't want to ask her why she thought that way. He didn't want to risk her saying that her return was all about him. That wasn't what she would have said because it wasn't totally true. Cris didn't feel like Dylan was the answer to all her happiness woes. She did feel like there was unfinished business between then, or rather, uncharted waters for them to conquer.

Dylan had spent the night, allowing the passion between them to be ignited again and again, without any misgivings. Of course, they didn't talk about what would happen after the sex, but that was okay for now. Cris still had a few things to smooth out on her end before that discussion became necessary.

Now, she turned from the window and surveyed the space once more. This was a huge master bedroom, with lots of natural light. She would love that for the lazy Sunday afternoons when she either binge-watched her favorite shows or relaxed with a good book. She walked through the room once more before moving out into the narrow hallway and eventually the open living/dining room and kitchen area where she stopped once more and looked around. Design ideas immediately popped into her mind and she knew that meant she was going to sign the lease for this apartment. She would have faith that one of the three interviews she'd had in the last two days would lead to a job offer and she would be able to afford the place.

She'd been carrying her purse on her left shoulder while holding her cell phone in her right hand to take pictures of the apartment. The phone buzzed in her hand. She lifted it so she could see the screen and smiled when she read Dylan's name at the top of the text message box.

6:00pm

That's all the message said.

Cris hadn't seen him in two days. They'd spoken on the phone a couple of times in the evening after he'd finished at work, but he hadn't come to the hotel again and he hadn't invited Cris to his place, or out anywhere. Dylan had always possessed an air of mystery. From his reluctance to talk in detail about his parents and his childhood, to what he truly wanted in his future, Cris had only received bits and pieces from him over the years. It appeared he hadn't lost that trait.

She cleared the message and noticed it was quarter to five now. She rushed out of the apartment noting she'd call the rental office first thing tomorrow morning to complete the application process. Right now, she needed to get showered and changed for whatever was happening at 6:oopm.

Twenty minutes later Cris walked into her hotel room and stopped immediately. On the table near the window was a huge black box with a white envelope taped to the top. Sitting in the chair next to the table were two black bags.

Eerie but intriguing. Cris walked toward the table and yanked the envelope off the box. She opened it to see a black card with no words on the front. Flipping the card over, she read the message: **Put on ONLY the dress and shoes. Don't be late. 6:00pm D**

Cris opened the box next and pulled back the lavender

tissue paper on top. Her gasp was audible as she stared down at the black dress. She touched the soft material of the dress, lifting it out of the box to hold it in front of her. It was a straight dress with a zipper down the front that would probably come to about mid-thigh. Cris pressed the dress against her and smiled. She was about to set the dress back into the box and go for the bags on the chair, but she noticed another layer of tissue paper, pink this time. She lay the black dress on the back of the second chair and pulled back the pink paper. There was another dress in the box. It was white in a pattern that looked like swatches of material wrapped around in an almost mummy-like fashion, with capped sleeves. There was a deep plunge in the back of this dress.

Cris recalled the message on the card.

"Yeah, I don't think anything else is going to fit with this dress," she whispered.

Seconds later, Cris was opening the two bags. Christian Louboutin shoes, one pair open-toed with a black and white striped tie at the ankle, the other pair patent leather closed-toe pumps that were black at the toe but faded into a black and white pattern from the middle to the five-inch heel.

She stood for another few seconds in awe of the packages before she realized Dylan was dressing her. He'd given her a time to be ready, the clothes to wear and an instruction to be on time. Butterflies danced in her stomach as she wondered what all this meant. That lasted for another five minutes before she had to dash into the shower.

Dylan sat at the table in the private room he'd reserved at The Corporation. It was actually a suite on the second of the four floors the club occupied in the Jefferson Swayne building. He brushed at imaginary lint on the lapel of his black suit jacket before letting his hands fall to his thighs.

He was nervous.

Dylan was never nervous.

He had a plan, but he wasn't sure it was going to work.

Dylan never doubted himself.

It was almost six fifteen. The driver should be pulling into the garage at this moment. He would park on the second floor, ride the private elevator with Cris and then leave her at the front desk. Once there, one of the evening hostesses would check her in on the guest registry. A text would come to Dylan's phone notifying him of her arrival and Cris would be escorted to his room.

Dinner would be served and then...he would show her what he really was. He wanted to be more nonchalant about what would happen and whether or not Cris liked what she learned, but he couldn't.

Was what he planned to do going to frighten Cris away once and for all? And was that what he really wanted, for her to walk out of his life, for good this time? It shouldn't matter if the answer to both questions was yes, Dylan didn't need anyone in his life on a personal basis. Isn't that what he'd been telling himself since his parents dropped him off in Chicago and jetted off to New Zealand?

His phone buzzed on the table. Dylan looked at the screen. Cris was on her way up.

Dylan stood. He fastened the single button on his suit

jacket and walked to the door. A few minutes later the door opened.

"Hello, Dylan." Cris walked in and looked around.

She wore the white dress and the shoes with the ties around her ankles. His dick jumped before Dylan could open his mouth to speak.

"Welcome to The Corporation." His voice sounded rugged with the words but she smiled in return.

Dylan moved around her to close the door.

He led her to the table and pushed her chair in when she was seated. The back of the dress was every bit more alluring than the front. He returned to the chair he'd been sitting in before she arrived, undid the button of his jacket and took a seat.

"You invited me here for dinner?" she asked with a nod to the expensive china dishes and crystal glasses that had been set on the black tablecloth.

"This club isn't just for sex," he replied.

"Really?" she lifted a brow and that's when he noticed how pretty she looked with the light layer of make-up she'd applied.

She'd also done something with her hair, pulling it to the side so that the curly ends fell over her left shoulder, while a sparkly clip held it in place.

"Do they have a menu or did you order for me?"

"I ordered for both of us," he told her. "Crab cakes, cole slaw and sweet potato fries."

Dylan recalled Tony recommending them, so he thought he'd give them a try, even if they were prepared by The Corporation's private caterers. When the food came, they ate in relative silence and when the dishes were cleared from the table, the server exited through a side door. Dylan stood and Cris looked up at him.

"I'm going to consider myself special because I know for a fact you don't have dinner with every woman you meet here."

Dylan didn't want to think of the other women he'd had here at the club. That's one of the reasons he'd requested a different suite tonight. Cris asked to be brought here and he'd obliged. Tonight wasn't going to be like any other night.

"You're nothing like any other woman I've ever known," he said with finality and walked to another door.

"Come with me," he said after opening the door and without turning back to her.

Dylan stepped into the other room. It was brighter here, with windows covered in tint so that no one on the outside could see in. There was a bed, nightstands and all the amenities of a master bedroom. There was also a wall of mirrors.

"So this is where the magic happens," she said.

Dylan turned to her. She was standing a few feet away from the bed, looking around as if she'd never seen a bedroom before. But that wasn't the problem. Dylan knew what she really wanted to know.

"I've never had another woman here, in this space," he told her. "You are the first."

She smiled and clasped her hands in front of her.

"I'm glad you picked the white one." Dylan liked both dresses and had imagined seeing her in them. But this one made her look almost angelic, until she turned around.

"I'm glad you like it," she said and did a slow spin so he could enjoy it once again.

Her entire back was bare, the material of the dress picking

up again just above the curve of her bottom. He wanted to kiss her there.

"Stand by the mirror," Dylan told her while he moved to a table and pulled open a drawer. He retrieved the ball gag he hadn't used on her before, a silk tie and a condom.

She had done as he instructed and was now watching him. Her gaze fell to what was in his hands and then returned to meet his.

"You want to know why I need this place and this lifestyle?" he asked. "It's because I know how it feels to be alone. I've grown accustom to it. This is the life that was meant for me."

"My parents thought they knew what my life was meant to be, but I went another way. You have a choice, Dylan. You can be and do whatever you want."

Hadn't he told himself that before? But nothing else had ever worked.

Instead of responding to her comment, Dylan leaned forward to drop a whisper-soft kiss on her lips. "Turn around."

She hesitated only a moment before doing as he said. Dylan stared at her through the mirror. He knew that face, those eyes, that nose, her smile. Everything about Cristine Palmer was etched permanently in his mind. Tonight would be an added memory, because it might be the last time he'd be with her.

Dylan dropped the items he held in his hand to the floor. If this was going to be the last time, he planned to make it worth it for both of them. While holding her gaze in the mirror, Dylan ran the back of his fingers down the skin left bare from her dress.

"I want you to think of nothing but pleasure," he whispered.

She licked her lips and shivered as his fingers brushed the small of her back.

"Imagine it washing over you like rain and rendering you helpless. I want you to give me every ounce of your pleasure tonight, Cris. Give it all to me."

She nodded. "I can do that."

She could give him her pleasure, but could he give her his? Could he give her something he'd never given another woman before?

Dylan unzipped the dress and decided he did not like the way his thoughts were drifting. He had to focus on the pleasure just as he'd instructed her to do. As lovely as the dress was on her, Dylan couldn't wait to get it off. He pushed the material from her shoulders and down until it hit the floor. She stepped out of it while Dylan's gaze remained fixated on her.

"You didn't wear anything under it," he said with a grateful sigh.

"I was instructed not to."

"And you listened. Good girl." He dropped a kiss to her bare shoulder, touching his tongue to her soft skin.

Her body was gorgeous. Trim, but curvy in all his favorite places.

"The reason I like the ball gag is not as a form of punishment, but because I found that focusing on the pleasure was easier without sound."

"Then why don't you wear one too?" she asked with an arch of her brow.

Dylan smirked at her through the mirror before kneeling to

grab the gag. "This is a small one since you're a beginner and it's pink, one of your favorite colors."

None of that had made her look at the gag with anything other than obvious skepticism.

Dylan fastened the apparatus around her head and was about to insert it before he paused, "If you want to stop, just say the word."

"I won't be able to say anything soon," she quipped.

"Which is why I'm giving you the chance now. And during, you can just shake your head no and I'll stop immediately. That's how this works, Cris. Either you're fully on board or we're done."

She inhaled slowly and released the breath while holding his gaze. "I'm fully in because this is what you think you need. It's a part of you I'm interested in learning more about, but you can be sure that if at any point I change my mind, I will definitely let you know."

Dylan believed her. He inserted the gag and brushed his fingers over her cheek when he was finished. He pulled her arms behind her back and tied them at her wrists before stepping back to stare at her. She looked lovely and sexy and his dick was so hard he almost shuddered from the pain.

He removed his jacket and unbuttoned his shirt, all while watching her standing in the mirror. Her eyes were growing darker with surprise and arousal. She was most likely surprised at how aroused she was becoming despite the items he used on her. Dylan was surprised at how aroused seeing her this way made him.

When he dropped his hands to the buckle of his belt, her

gaze lowered. Her chest did a quick rise and fall. She shifted her weight on her feet, rubbing her thighs together.

"Are you ready for me so soon?" he asked.

She did not reply, but continued to watch.

Her nipples were hard. It wasn't warm in the room, but it wasn't cold either. Dylan undid the belt, the button on his pants and the zipper. He pushed them down his long legs and stepped out of his shoes before taking them off. He'd purposely left his boxers on because he normally did not remove them at all. He could pull his dick through the slit in the material, sheath himself and fuck just fine with them on.

He came to stand behind her, reaching his hands around to cup her breasts. The feel of the weight of her breasts in his hands was glorious, the sight of his flesh on her flesh in such an intimate way was mouthwatering. He wanted to go slow. He normally did. But tonight, this time, he wasn't going to be able to.

One hand slid down her torso to rest over her navel. They looked like an erotic portrait, two toned black bodies and two sets of eyes clouded by desire. It was an amazing and alluring sight. Her legs parted even before Dylan began to move his hand again. She sighed and let her head fall back against his shoulder. Dylan dropped his head and kissed her neck. He pressed his fingers further until they separated the folds of her pussy. He touched her clit and she arched against him. Two fingers inside her and Dylan was lost. His tongue moved along the skin of her neck while he pumped in and out of her.

Ragged moans escaped him. His dick was so hard it poked right through the slit in his boxers to poke against her back. He pressed into her because he was ready to fuck.

"I've never craved a woman before." For a moment Dylan wasn't sure who was speaking.

The voice didn't sound like his and the words weren't something he would say to anyone.

"I cannot stop thinking about you, Cristine. About touching you, tasting you and..."

He squeezed her breast and pumped his fingers into her faster. Pulling his fingers out momentarily he rubbed them along her clit before dipping them back inside. She bent her knees and thrust her hips against his fingers. Her head was still resting on his shoulder.

"Look at me!" Dylan yelled. "Look at us!"

Her head jerked up and she met his gaze with a wide-eyed stare.

"Is this what you came back for, Cristine? To be in this room with me? To give me everything I require? Is that what you want in your life?"

It was what Dylan wanted in his. This pleasure. This comfort. This intense feeling that he'd never experienced before.

She did not respond. Not a moan or nod of her head. Nothing.

Dylan pulled his fingers from her. He released her breast and stepped away from her. He wanted to feel his skin against hers, so he quickly pushed the boxers down his legs and knelt down to pick up the condom packet he'd dropped on the floor. When he was once again standing, Dylan caught Cris's gaze through the mirror. He began sheathing himself while she watched his hand holding his dick, smoothing the condom over his length, but she did not...could not speak. What would she say if she could speak? Was it something he would want to hear?

Focus.

Dylan moved to stand directly behind her again. He wrapped an arm around her waist and stepped forward to ease her closer to the mirror until her breasts touched the glass. Then Dylan positioned himself. He pressed his dick between the crease in her ass and moved lower until his head touched the mouth of her opening. He thrust hard, embedding his full length into her. She did not make a sound but moved until her forehead touched the glass as well.

Dylan closed his eyes and began pumping into her. He grabbed the tie that was binding her hands for leverage and buried himself in her, pulling out and thrusting in once again. Pleasure washed over him like heavy waves and he gritted his teeth against the intensity of the feeling. When that wasn't enough he moaned. A low sound at first and then as his pumping increased, and the pleasure became too much for him to hold under wraps, he groaned loud.

"Look at me!" he yelled again. "Look at us!"

But Cris did not look at him through the mirror this time. She looked over her shoulder until she found and held his gaze. She didn't have to speak to tell Dylan what he knew without a doubt. His entire body froze because in that moment he knew that Cris had seen him. She'd finally seen the real Dylan James.

8

*C*ris shook the managing partner's hand. She kept her smile in place and told herself not to turn around to catch the lecherous snob watching her ass as she walked out of his office. After she stepped inside the elevator she sighed heavily. This was interview number seven. The last four had taken place in the two weeks since she'd been invited to The Corporation by Dylan.

He'd offered his help in getting her a position, but Cris turned him down. She'd gotten her first job on her own, she was certain she could get another. In fact, she already had an offer. It was at a medium-size firm leading their transactional law department, something she was more than qualified to do. Actually, it was the job she'd first wanted at the firm in New York, but after years of proving herself to the partners there, Cris had soon realized they never intended to let her—a black woman who hadn't attended an Ivy League college or law school—lead one of their largest departments. In essence, they didn't want her leading a group of fourteen white men who had gone to the "right" schools and had the "right" background. That had been the start of her re-evaluation of what she wanted from life.

Now, after leaving her high six-figure-paying job, returning the Mercedes she'd been leasing and once again refusing to use any of the money her parents had put into a trust fund for her, she was starting all over again. And she wasn't one hundred percent positive that the offer to work at a smaller firm, making thirty-five thousand less than she had been in New York, while doing almost, if not, more work, was a viable solution. Which meant, she was still looking for a job. She was also still staying at the hotel because without an employer to verify employment or paystubs to provide, no apartment building or landlord was going to offer her a lease. It wasn't yet time to panic. She was certain of that, or at least she was doing a damn good job of convincing herself.

Besides, even if she hadn't found a job yet, Cris was certain she'd found something else—her soulmate. After that night at The Corporation her "just friends" relationship with Dylan was officially gone. They'd slipped into being lovers and great friends and for the last two weeks their dinners, nights full of lovemaking, shared breakfasts and daily text messages had confirmed what she'd dared to dream, that she was in love with her best friend.

It sounded so cliché and it was something that nine years ago neither of them would have considered. And yet it was something so right. Every part of her mind, body and soul knew that being with him was exactly what she needed. As for Dylan, well Cris wasn't so sure he was ready to admit the same thing. While she now knew about the secret of his dark sexual desires, and enjoyed most of them—the rope tying he'd done the other night was not her favorite—she was still acutely aware of the part of himself that Dylan still held back from her. In the past couple of weeks they'd talked about his parents and their current political status, his work at his firm and where he envisioned himself five years from now. They'd even talked a little about a rent dispute issue he'd discovered while looking into the Southlake Restoration Project. This issue didn't involve Southlake, but it did concern another neighborhood in Chicago. Dylan was actually planning a trip back to Chicago before the end of the year to meet with the local representatives. Cris thought that was an excellent idea. She could see the need for legislative reform in the area. She'd also done a little background checking on the types of businesses in the areas around Southlake and how they could benefit from better organization in the future. And while all of this was great progress in their new relationship, Cris was very aware of the fact that in the weeks she'd been back in Washington, D.C.—minus the night in the beginning when she'd followed him from work to his apartment building—Dylan had never invited her to his home. The night of their auction date he'd taken her to his playroom. Their next tryst had been at her hotel room and then they'd gone to The Corporation. In the past two weeks they either spent the night at her hotel or at the club, and each time after an early morning breakfast, he rushed back to his place to change and head to the office.

It wasn't time to worry about that either. It was still very early in their revised relationship. They hadn't even given the relationship a name. Was she his bae? Was he hers? Were there rules and boundaries they should be keeping in mind as they proceeded? Did this have a chance at ending in marriage? For Cris, the answer to most of those questions was a resounding yes, but she wasn't so sure about Dylan. In fact, she had no clue how he felt about any of that. And she was actually tired of thinking about it right now.

It was a crisp fall day in the city and the minute she'd stepped off the elevator, walked along the marbled floors of the lobby and through the glass front doors of the building, a brisk wind slapped her in the face. She adjusted her purse on her arm and pulled her wool cooper-colored coat tighter over her chest. The loose curls she'd used the flat iron to put in her hair earlier today were now blowing in the wind as she walked down the street. She decided she wasn't ready to go back to her hotel yet. It was a little after five and instead she wanted to walk and clear her mind for a while.

Three blocks later, the brisk fall air had turned chilly and Cris craved a cup of hot chocolate. Or she'd seen the coffee shop sign in the distance ahead and told herself that would be a good place to get warm and get off her feet. The natural-colored four-inch heel knee boots she'd worn to match the beige wool skirt suit, weren't exactly the best walking shoes.

Minutes later she was inside the coffee shop, shivering slightly. She stood in the line and ordered hot chocolate and two huge oatmeal raisin cookies before finding a seat near the window. Cris had removed her coat, plugged her phone into a wall charger next to the table and was scrolling through her emails while sipping her hot chocolate when she was interrupted.

"Hey girl! I was wondering when we were going to run into each other again."

Tisha McQueen, Cris's former grad-school roommate was standing beside the table removing her black leather coat.

"Hey," Cris said a lot less enthusiastically than Tisha had spoken. She watched Tisha put her coat on the back of the empty chair across from her as if she'd been invited to stay.

"Winter is definitely coming," Tisha continued as she rubbed her hands together and lifted them to her mouth to blow into them. "I'm gonna get me a coffee. I'll be right back."

Cris watched in confusion as Tisha walked away. A few inches taller than Cris, Tisha had a deep sepia complexion and wore her auburn-dyed hair in a short pixie cut. That and a few extra pounds that looked very good on her, were the only things that had changed since Cris had seen Tisha years ago.

"So I've been wanting to catch up with you for a couple weeks now," Tisha said when she was back at the table with her coffee and chocolate chip muffin.

"Really? You still have my number right? Because I think Garrett said you gave it to him." Try as she might Cris wasn't able to hide the sarcastic tone of her comments. The only reason Tisha had her number was because the day after she was back in town, Cris had run into her at the bookstore they used to love visiting when they were at Howard. That little reunion and number exchange had led to Tisha passing Cris's number along to Garrett and that had led to the date during which Cris had to put her ex-boyfriend in his place. So yeah, she had some feelings about that.

Tisha shrug and broke her muffin apart. "You two were together for two years. He was the love of your life or at least that's how you acted during freshman and sophomore year. So when I told him you were back and he said he wanted to link up with you, I thought finally, they can get their act together."

"You were never a good matchmaker," Cris quipped and picked up her cup to take another sip. Maybe if she kept eating and drinking she wouldn't have to entertain this conversation.

"Anyway, he told me about your date and I gotta say I'm disappointed."

Cris broke a piece of cookie and stuck it into her mouth to keep from responding.

"It's been a long time since we were in school, Cris. And damn, we were kids back then. All of us made mistakes. You remember that night me and Richmond asked Dylan to be a third in our bed? Girl, I'm not even trying no mess like that these days." Tisha chewed her muffin like it was spare ribs at a cook-out, the look on her face was absolutely blissful.

"I'm aware that people can grow and change in time. I also know what my expectations are for any man in my life. Garrett cannot meet those expectations."

"And you think Dylan can?" Tisha's brows lifted while she sipped from her cup and watched Cris for a response.

That's why Cris waited a beat before responding. Her knee-jerk reaction was to read Tisha for all she was worth—which at this moment was pure trash.

"What I think is that I'll be selecting the men in my life. I do not need you or anyone else pushing me and some guy together."

"Garrett's not some guy," Tisha corrected. "He's a guy you spent two years with. You two know everything about each other. You were the perfect couple."

"He cheated on me," Cris said blandly. "Twice."

"Kids grow up and out of childish ways."

"I'm not interested in taking another chance with him. I'm not interested in Garrett on that level at all. So if he's paying you for your matchmaking services, you might as well terminate that contract."

Cris was through with this strange conversation. She slipped her last cookie into the small bag they'd come in and dropped it into her purse. She was turning in the chair to reach for her coat when Tisha's next words stopped her.

"You like leading guys around on a leash don't you? It's a part of that southern charm masked as control you learned from growing up in South Carolina as part of a rich family." Tisha stuffed another piece of muffin in her mouth as she nodded. "You always did think you were better than the rest of us because your daddy owned an insurance company. Well, you didn't think you were better than Dylan, but I'm sure your father didn't envision his baby girl marrying a politician's son. At least not until that senator had been named to a high profile committee and has been looked at for the next democratic presidential nominee."

Cris did not speak.

Tisha smiled as she finished chewing. "Yeah, I know what you're up to. You don't want to settle for Garrett when you can snag the big fish this time. See, when we were in college you wanted to keep your options open. Why else would you head to New York to go to Syracuse, of all law schools, when you could have easily gone to Maryland with Dylan or stayed at Howard with Garrett and I? Now, after not clinching a partnership at that big 'ole firm in New York, you run back here to see if your leash around Dylan's neck is still tight enough to rein him in."

"Why would I do that, Tisha? I mean, you seem to know so much about me. Tell me why I would come back for Dylan instead of going home to South Carolina where there is more than one rich black man that I can surely hook up with?"

"Because Dylan's still the bigger fish. He's the one you let get away and the fabulous Cristine Palmer cannot possibly afford another disappointment like the professional one you had in New York. See, I know you, Cris. I know you better than anybody else in this city."

Cris stood. She yanked her coat off the chair and grabbed her purse. "You don't know a damn thing, Tisha. Just like you didn't know squat in undergrad and cheated your way into law school where you could barely hold onto to an average GPA. That's why you're working as an associate in a personal injury firm now, because that's about as high as your average ass can aim."

Cris left the coffee shop before Tisha could respond. She pushed her arms into her coat and walked quickly down to the next block where she finally pulled out her phone and called for an Uber. As she waited, she tried everything from breathing to counting backward from one hundred to calm herself down. No way was she going to remain upset by Tisha's ridiculous accusations.

Even if she wondered if a small part of what the irritating woman said was true.

Dylan hadn't wanted to attend the meeting of the Young Black Lawyers Association. He'd been at work since seven in the morning and the meeting didn't start until six-thirty. But now that it was over, Dylan was glad that he'd come. After taking care of the items on the agenda, Dylan had the opportunity to talk to a few attorneys who had more experience than he did in landlord/tenant issues and drafting effective legislation on rent reform. This information would be invaluable when he traveled back to Chicago to meet with the representatives in a few weeks. What had started out as a way to further assist Mama Peaches and her project, had turned into a totally new project. Century Heights was a predominantly black neighborhood located a short distance from Southlake. Researching the rent issues in that area had begun to take up more of Dylan's time. But that wasn't a bad thing. In fact, Dylan was really enjoying working through the problem and his plans to help in Southlake. Even though lobbying for new legislation was part of his work at the firm, this had taken on a personal quality to him. Finding a way to permanently help residents and business owners stay and prosper in this other Chicago neighborhood.

"Great, so I'll call your office tomorrow to get on your calendar for next week. I know that's the earliest time I have available. We can talk more about the policies already in place here in comparison to a much larger city like Chicago."

"That'll work," Dylan replied.

He was talking to Winston Hinkle who used to work at a large firm in Baltimore, but had started his own firm in D.C. a year ago.

Dylan was looking down at his calendar displayed on his phone as he spoke. "Next week's better for me too. I want to have a firm presentation in place for when I meet with the representatives in a couple of weeks."

"Sure, that makes sense. You'll be able to use statistics compiled in the Baltimore and D.C. metropolitan areas to make your case for Chicago. The size may not be comparable but when you factor in the amount of small black owned businesses and black residents in the Century Heights area, you're almost spot-on for the change that's required," Winston continued.

Dylan nodded. "That's what I was thinking too. Thanks for your help with this, man. I appreciate it."

Dylan closed out his calendar and slipped his phone into his pocket. He reached out a hand to Winston who immediately accepted and shook.

"Don't mention it. This is what we went to school for, to help our communities. It's why I left to start my own firm where I could truly focus on that goal. But you've got the Loman Regent name behind you. Not to mention your dad being a senator. That's going to go a long way toward getting the lawmakers' attention when you get out there."

Dylan nodded as they released hands. He had no intention of mentioning his father's name, but he would definitely tell them which firm he was currently working for, even though the Southlake Association was not an official client. He would work out that detail later, for now, he was glad he'd made the connection with Winston and was going to gather further information.

"Hey. You two having a private meeting?" Garrett asked as he approached them.

Dylan's demeanor instantly soured.

Winston shook his head. "Not at all. Just catching up with

an old classmate," he said. "But I've gotta run. My fiance's holding dinner for me so I've got to get going. Nice seeing you, Garrett. Dylan, we'll link up next week."

Dylan nodded. "Sure thing. Have a good one."

Garrett barely said goodbye to Winston before he turned to Dylan. "So Winston's trying to come on board at your firm? I thought he'd branched out on his own."

The last person in this room with at least thirty-five young black attorneys, that Dylan wanted to speak to was Garrett. He'd spotted Garrett sitting at another table when he'd first entered the meeting and while there were empty seats at that table Dylan had found someplace else to sit. He wasn't avoiding the guy, because that would give him too much importance, but he didn't have time to waste talking to him either.

"That's not what we were speaking about." Dylan replied and was about to turn and walk away, but Garrett touched a hand to his shoulder to stop him.

Dylan looked down at that hand and then back up to Garrett. The guy quickly answered the silently spoken question by pulling his hand away just as fast.

"Well, I wanted to talk to you about something," Garrett began. "I'm not cut out to be a lobbyist like you and Winston, but I'm a fantastic litigation attorney. And I hear Loman Regent is looking to fill a few associate positions."

"They're first year associate positions," Dylan replied dryly. "You've been practicing for at least four years."

There'd been a lag in Garrett completing law school, so that he graduated long after Dylan had. Whether that was for a financial or academic reason, Dylan wasn't sure and he didn't care.

"I'm not too proud to start on the ground floor of such a prestigious firm. Especially not if someone is willing to sponsor me."

And apparently he wasn't too proud to make an ass out of himself. Did Garrett really think Dylan was going to recommend him for a job with his firm?

"Not if that someone is me." Dylan figured it was best to just get that answer out there.

"Whoa, you so fast to hold a brotha' down?"

Dylan wanted to sigh with consternation. Instead he took a deep, slow breath and replied, "I cannot in good conscience recommend you for a job. That's not holding you down, that's standing up for what I believe."

Dylan knew from the way Garrett screwed up his face that this conversation was about to take a bad turn.

"What's that supposed to mean? I have a good litigation record with my firm. I'm just looking for the next step in my career."

Dylan shrugged. "That's understandable, but I'm not the one to help you in that regard."

Dylan did turn away this time, but Garrett was persistent. He wasn't totally stupid either, instead of touching Dylan again, Garrett hurriedly skirted around him so that he was now blocking Dylan's path.

"You can't call up someone in your human resources department and talk to them for five minutes about me? Or hell, you can't even forward my resume to HR? Are you serious?"

"I'm dead serious," Dylan told him and wondered why this man found that so hard to believe.

"What happened to all that pro-black stuff you were just clapping for a few minutes ago? I mean isn't that what this group is all about, helping black attorneys in the D.C. area rise and succeed?"

"It is. And there are many more black people who can help you. But I'm not one of them. Now, I'm leaving." Dylan hoped if he said it this time Garrett would get the picture and back the hell up.

He did not. Instead he puffed up his chest and stared directly into Dylan's eyes.

"You ain't shit," he spat. "I knew that back in college when you thought you were too good to socialize with us at the house and I know it even more now since you tried to ambush my date with Cris a couple weeks ago."

Dylan gave into a feeling he didn't normally entertain. He took a step forward causing Garrett to take one back to keep them from actually touching.

"You didn't deserve her back then and you certainly don't deserve her now," he told him through clenched teeth. "Aside from that you have two reports to the Attorney Grievance Commission in the last six months, including one where you got a little too touchy with a female client. So no, I will never recommend you for a job at my firm or any other firm. And I will definitely warn any woman I know against dating a lying, cheating bastard like you."

That should have been enough. Dylan should have walked away then and not looked back. But the memory of Garrett sitting across the table looking smug and like he was only hours away from taking Cris to his bed that night at Tony's flashed in Dylan's mind. Her grabbed Garrett by the lapel of his suit and pulled him so that they were almost nose-to-nose now.

"And if you so much as breathe her name again I'll make you eat your teeth."

Dylan let go of Garrett's jacket and pushed him so hard the guy stumbled back a few steps. He gave him one last look of contempt before turning and this time walking out of the room.

9

*D*ylan was quieter than usual during their dinner the next night. Cris had suggested the restaurant and time by texting him mid-afternoon. She'd just decided to turn down the job she'd been offered and wanted to talk to someone about the decision. Dylan had been the first person to come to mind. Besides, she hadn't seen him yesterday because he'd had a meeting after work and he hadn't called her when that meeting was over. That was just as well because Cris's head had still been spinning after the conversation with Tisha, which meant she wasn't in the mood for company anyway.

"So, I think I'm okay with my decision to not take the job. I mean, I guess I have to be okay with it now, since I already replied to the hiring partner. I just didn't feel like it was the right place or maybe even the right position for me." They'd just finished their meal and Cris insisted they also get dessert. This place had the best carrot cake, which was mainly the reason she'd suggested it. She also did not want Dylan to continue staring into space like he didn't know if he were coming or going, so she was doing everything she could to keep the conversation flowing.

"If it's not the right position for you, then why are you continuing to interview at so many firms? The bulk of your experience is as a transactional attorney. You've made your name in that area of law already so it's no wonder they offered you the job."

Good, at least he replied. She'd asked a number of basic "how was your day?", "are you enjoying the weather?" questions during the meal, to which she'd received the briefest of answers. Now, it appeared they may actually have a conversation.

"I know. I think that's what I'm struggling with. I didn't like having to start working on insurance defense cases, especially since my father owns an insurance company. But I knew that was a means to an end. Now, I'm not sure transactional law is all I want to be doing with the rest of my career."

He stared at her from across the table. His goatee had grown in thicker in the weeks since she'd been back. Cris hadn't realized how much she liked Dylan with a goatee. It made him look more distinguished than sexy, even though he still possessed those heartbreaker good looks that had all the women on campus crushing on him years ago. Women who included Tisha. That thought hadn't been lost on Cris as she'd replayed her conversation with her former roommate last night.

"If you don't do transactional law, what else would you like to do?" he asked. "There are some openings at my firm, but they're entry level association positions. I could talk to a few people to get a feel for what might be available as more of a lateral move for you."

"No," she replied instantly. Tisha's comments about Cris having Dylan on a leash while she decided if he was good enough for her or not, was still prevalent in her mind as well. "I mean, I don't want to be walked into a firm on your word."

Especially not now that she was sleeping with him.

"Last night I was actually thinking that I might be going about this all wrong. I keep looking for a firm where I can fit in. but what if my calling is to actually make a place for myself?"

Dylan didn't answer right away.

"When I was young I remember my dad telling my brothers about all the little jobs he held while he was in college. And then when he graduated from college with a business degree, how hard it still was for him to find a job. Speaking of my dad, his 60th birthday celebration is coming up at the end of the month. If you're not busy, it would be great to have a date for the party."

"Times have changed since then, Cris. Besides, you also have a law degree and an excellent track record with domestic and international clients. But I hear you about making a place for yourself. That's what my mother did. She created the type of company she wanted to work at, a sort of temp agency for international attorneys. This allowed her to travel with my father and still maintain her own career."

"That's exactly what I'm thinking!" she replied with an excited smile. The smile was two-fold because at that exact moment the waiter had also brought her carrot cake to the table.

"So you want to start your own firm? Do you have capital for that? What about starter clients? Anyone from your former firm you think you could lure over to start you out?"

Dylan had ordered a slice of double chocolate cake, even though he'd told her he was only ordering it so she wouldn't have to eat alone. Cris had no problem eating alone, but she let him have his excuse. He used his fork to cut a small square before putting it into his mouth.

"I haven't thought that far yet. I mean I want to really mull this over because starting over at thirty is bound to be a hell of a lot easier than starting over at forty. So I want to be sure that this is the actual next step for me and that it's something I can see myself doing until it's time to retire."

Dylan nodded as she took her first and second bite of the carrot cake. He finished chewing his cake and sat back in the chair.

"What?" she asked when he hadn't said anything after she'd taken a few more bites, but had only stared at her.

"So is that what this is about? You came back to D.C. to figure out your future?"

His tone was a little dry, but Cris didn't want to read too much into it.

Cris set her fork down and wiped her fingers and mouth with her napkin. She put that down and sat back in her chair the same way Dylan was doing. "I came back to D.C. because I felt I had unfinished business here."

"Unfinished business that included me and Garrett?"

"Garrett? Oh you mean that night at Tony's? Tisha gave him my number. I did not look him up as soon as I came back if that's what you're thinking."

"But you did agree to go out with him?"

"Yes, I did. Because I was thinking of networking with other attorneys. Garrett was always on the social scene so I figured he'd know about the best networking events for me to get to know the lawyers around here. Wait, are you angry because I went to dinner with Garrett over two weeks ago?" It didn't seem like Dylan. He wasn't the jealous type. Mainly because he wasn't the commit to a woman type. This was a known fact when they were in college but she'd been trying to convince herself that maybe he'd changed over time.

"I'm not angry," he said but the words were spoken tightly and the muscle that always twitched in his jaw when he was irritated, was twitching. "I'm just trying to figure out why you would give him the time of day after all he put you through."

"I gave him time on a business level. That dinner was never supposed to be anything personal, for me at least."

"But not for him. You don't have to tell me because I already know. He wants you back. Who wouldn't?"

Okay, now she was confused. Was he jealous? Did he not want her with Garrett because he wanted her all to himself? That was silly. Didn't he know she was already with him, which was exactly where she suspected she was always meant to be? Maybe she should tell him.

"Hey, why don't we finish up here and head back to my hotel," she said. "Or we can go to your place if you prefer?"

Now that wasn't too obvious. But the words had fell from her lips before she could stop them. Hell, Cris had no idea what was going on this evening. Dylan was acting weird and she seemed to be saying all the wrong things. Was it a full moon or some other such nonsense? What happened to the easy conversations they were used to having, or even the simmering passion that had been getting them through the last two weeks?

"No. Not tonight," he answered. "I'll take you home. I have

something I need to work on tonight and then I need to be at the office early tomorrow morning."

Cris could have pressed the issue. She could have asked why he hadn't invited her to his house or where this thing with them was going. But she didn't. Partly because she had other stuff on her mind as well. She was being totally truthful when she told Dylan and Tisha that she did not come back to D.C. solely for him. Her return was based on a need that she felt wasn't being fulfilled. If Dylan filled part of that need, that was cool. But Cris had never been the type of woman to base her entire existence on a man.

"That's fine. I have some things to work out as well." She pushed her plate with the half eaten cake away and signaled to the waiter that they were ready for the check.

When the check was set on the table, Cris quickly scooped up the holder and stuffed her credit card inside before giving it to the waiter. Dylan had reached for his wallet, but she was faster. Not only did she not need a man to complete her, she also didn't need him to pay for her dinner. Especially not if he was still contemplating whether or not to invite her to his house.

She had stood and was pulling her coat on when the waiter came back with her card. Cris signed the receipt and grabbed her purse.

"I'll drive you back to the hotel," Dylan said when he stood and pushed his arms through his jacket.

"Okay," she said with a shrug. "I'll meet you out front."

Walking away from him at that moment was needed. The conflict brewing inside of her where Dylan was concerned was growing and she knew that sooner, rather than later, she would need some definition for what they were doing. She'd never been an affair type of woman and she wasn't about to start now. If Dylan needed a little more time and space to get his head together, she could spare that while she worked on her future business plan. But she wasn't going to wait forever. No matter how strongly she believed she and Dylan were meant to be, she had no intention of forcing him into something he did not want.

***

Dylan cursed and rubbed his hands down his face the moment he closed the door to his apartment. He stood in that spot with his eyes closed, taking slow and steady breaths as he tried to figure out what the hell he was doing.

He should never have agreed to have dinner with Cris. Not when he was still seething from his run-in with Garrett last night. He should have just given her some excuse and come straight home tonight. But a big part of him wanted to see her. He'd missed seeing her yesterday. That didn't make any sense either.

Dylan pulled his jacket off and hung it in the closet. He walked further into his apartment passing the bar where he usually fixed himself a nightly rum and coke. Tonight he headed straight to the couch which faced the windows in his living room. Sitting down heavily, he leaned forward and rested his elbows on his knees.

"What are you doing?"

The words fell into the quiet room. Dylan looked straight ahead and through the windows to the city view. He loved living in D.C. This was where he belonged. It had taken him a while to figure that out because all his childhood years had been spent traveling across the globe. He enjoyed his job and was proud of some of the legislation he'd helped put into place. He was successful and happy with the way his life turned out.

Or at least he had been before Cris came back.

He could actually take that back a little further. Dylan had felt content until the moment he'd talked to Mama Peaches. Hearing her voice again had immediately taken him back to a time he'd never thought he'd miss. There'd been five other boys living with her when Dylan arrived and they'd all treated him like he was family. Except Dylan didn't know how to act in a family. He'd never had one. Living and traveling with his parents was like an arrangement he'd had no control over.

It was no wonder he'd been feeling off a few days after receiving that call. All the years it had taken him to establish himself and put down roots in this place—the place of his choosing—and with one phone call he'd immediately started questioning his decisions. Dylan had needed the release that he could only get at the club that night. Sure, he'd seen the strange number calling his phone and he'd ignored. But then she'd texted him from that strange number and he'd known she was back. Only Dylan didn't want her to be back. He hadn't wanted another blast from his past because he was already settled in what he'd planned for his future.

And then she was at the club.

Dylan dropped his head and stared down at the floor.

Everything had spiraled out of control from that point on and now he was having an affair with his closest friend. That didn't sound as bad as he'd knew it was. Didn't everyone want to be in love with their best friend? He supposed so even though Dylan had never been a romantic, nor had he believed in happy ever after. But this was wrong because he knew there was no way he could give Cris what she wanted, what she deserved.

He jumped up.

"That's enough!"

As if saying it aloud was going to make letting this situation go any easier.

Dylan shook his shoulders and rotated his neck. He walked back into his bedroom and changed his clothes. When he returned to the living room he was wearing sweatpants and a t-shirt, his bare feet padding across the hard wood floors. He closed the blinds in the living room and went to the kitchen to grab a bottled water instead of the drink he desperately needed. From there he went into his office and was booting up his computer when his cell phone buzzed.

He'd slipped it into the front pocket of his sweatpants and now pulled it out to see that he'd received a text message from another strange number.

You might want to re-think not helping me get into your firm. I'm sure your father's presidential election campaign manager won't like seeing these.

Dylan swiped down on the phone to see one picture after another of him and Cris going into and leaving out of The Corporation. There was even a picture inside the club when one of the women had come to them offering to be a third for the evening. Dylan recalled that night, the woman had been very chummy and instead of being freaked out by the thought of a ménage, Cris had calmly told the woman that she could handle Dylan by herself. That had been the moment Dylan knew he'd completely fallen for Cristine Palmer.

With a loud curse Dylan tossed the phone across the room because not only had he fallen, but now it seemed his mistakes were going to drag his father down as well.

10

"My name is Gwen. It's a pleasure to meet you, Cris."

Cris accepted the woman's hand and returned her smile. "Hi Gwen. It's nice to meet you too."

"I know he was on a conference call a few minutes ago, but the light's off so he's finished now. I'll take you in."

It was a little after noon and Cris had decided at the spur of the moment to come to Dylan's office. She walked behind the woman toward his office and hoped he was in a better mood than he had been last night. He hadn't called or sent a text to her since then and she'd remained silent on her end as well, giving him that space she thought he might need. But she was very excited about what she'd decided in the wee hours of the morning and she couldn't wait to share it with him.

"Dylan, I'm bringing you a bit of sunshine on this dreary Wednesday afternoon," Gwen announced after a quick knock on Dylan's door and pushing it open.

She walked swiftly into the space and Cris obediently

followed, stopping at one of the guest chairs across from Dylan's desk. He was sitting in the chair behind his desk, but it was turned in the direction of the window so she could not immediately see her face. Or, more importantly, he hadn't seen hers. But when he turned around, his expression said it all—he was not in a better mood.

"What are you doing here?" he immediately asked.

"Is that anyway to greet a nice woman who came to take you to lunch?" Gwen asked.

Cris hadn't said anything about lunch.

"I was in the area and I had something I wanted to discuss with you," was Cris simple reply.

"And you should stop being so testy to pretty women who come for a visit," Gwen chastised him.

Dylan looked to the older woman and took a deep breath before saying whatever he'd been about to say.

"You're right, Gwen. Thanks for escorting her in," he said and Cris was astonished.

There was someone in this world that could actually bring Dylan down a notch. She was going to remember to send Gwen flowers.

"Right. Now, you don't have anything on your schedule until three this afternoon, so take her some place nice for a long lunch." Gwen turned away from Dylan and winked at Cris as she turned to leave the office.

Cris waited until she heard the door close behind her before she spoke.

"I really didn't mean to interrupt. If you're busy it can wait until tonight."

"Did we have plans for tonight?"

"No," she answered.

Dylan sighed. "Look, I just don't usually have women coming to the office. In fact, nobody has ever come to the office to see me on a personal basis and I'd like to keep it that way. The partners are real sticklers for no fraternizing at work."

Cris could feel herself losing the last shreds of her patience with him.

"I didn't come here so you could fuck me on the desk, Dylan. I came to share some news with you. But if you're too busy to hear it, that's fine I can go."

"I didn't say that," he told her and stood. "I'm just saying that maybe you could have called first."

Cris gave him a curt nod. "You're right. You are at work, so I should have called first. I'll just leave and catch up with you later."

She had turned and was on her way to the door when Dylan touched her arm.

"That's not what I meant," he said and shook his head.

"Then what did you mean, Dylan? And while you're answering that question, why don't you tell me what the hell is going on because this volleying back and forth with you is giving me whiplash." Her patience had officially left the building!

He let his fingers linger on her arm but did not speak.

"There's just a lot going on. I thought I had this under control but obviously not."

"What are you talking about?" Cris wanted to know and then again, she didn't. If he was having trouble figuring things out, she could do it for him.

"Look, Dylan. We don't have to do this if it's not what you

want. I told you I thought there was something between us that we'd left unexplored years ago and I thought we were giving it a try now. But if it's not what you want, fine. All you have to do is say that. I'm not in the habit of keeping men who don't want to be kept."

If it were at all possible he looked even angrier at her words. "And I'm not in the habit of being kept, by anyone."

"Okay," she said with a heavy sigh. "Then that's that. I guess I'll be seeing you around in the networking circles then."

"Oh, you mean the way Garrett ran into me the other night to ask for a job?"

"What? When did Garrett ask you for a job and what did you tell him?"

"I told him hell no, I'd never refer him for a job. And then he decided blackmail was a better tactic!"

Dylan went back to his desk to grab his cell phone. He swiped over it and thrust it in front of Cris's face so she could read the screen.

She sucked in a breath. That was the first reaction she could manage.

"He's an ass," she finally managed to say.

"Yeah, an ass that can now use the pictures to not only compromise my father's upcoming campaign, but will most certainly cost me my job here at the firm. The partners are not going to take kindly to the fact that one of their supervising attorneys' frequents a sex club!"

Cris swiped through each of the pictures before handing the phone back to Dylan. Now she understood his mood. For Dylan, everything was about his job and his reputation. Those were the only things he had control over. He'd told her that on many occasions when they were in school. That's why he'd chosen to focus on his coursework and not personal relationships. His parents had done the same in their lives. They'd decided what their professional goals were going to be and they'd worked toward them, even after they had a son. In doing that, Dylan never had the opportunity to experience a real home with a family who loved and supported him even if he grew up and followed a blue collar career path.

"Why did you tell Garrett you wouldn't help him get a job? I mean, don't get me wrong, the mere fact that he's pulling this stunt proves how much of an idiot he is, but I'm guessing this is more personal for you." Cris had never seen Dylan this upset before.

Not only was his brow furrowed, but his body was tense, his fingers clenching at his side. He was staring at her intently, almost accusatorily, but Cris was determined to stay calm. Her strategy in all her cases, as well as when dealing with her share of family disagreements, was to always gather as many answers as she could to key questions. From there she could assess the whole situation and decide how best to proceed. Thinking about this in such a formal manner was definitely keeping her from going off on her own emotional tangent.

Dylan accepted the phone and locked its screen. He slipped it back into his pocket and moved a few steps away from her until his backside was leaning against the edge of his desk.

"Because like I told you last night, he wants you back. I knew that when I saw you at dinner with him. I remembered everything he did to you when we were in school and I couldn't for the life of me figure out why you'd put yourself in that position again. I mean, you have everything going for you now. Your career is on the right track, you're brilliant and beautiful, definitely too much to be dealing with the likes of Garrett. So when I saw him at the meeting the night before last and he asked me to put in a good word for him, I told him no. He's an opportunistic leach who cannot be trusted."

"That night I went to dinner with him, is that why you came to my hotel room and spent the night with me? Because you wanted to make sure I didn't go back to Garrett?" That hadn't been Cris's original line of thought when this conversation began but as she'd listened to Dylan talk some things had begun to click into place. "Taking me to The Corporation and spending all this time with me was your way of getting me away from Garrett? It had nothing to do with what you wanted for us right now or possibly in the future?"

She could tell that her questions were taking Dylan off guard. He'd blinked quickly and then looked away with an exasperated sigh.

"So now because you want to make sure Garrett doesn't get me or the job, you find yourself in the center of what could be a professionally disastrous blackmail scheme for you and your father."

"You're in the pictures too, Cris. How do you think prospective firms are going to look at you when you apply to them now? This could hurt both of us all because I couldn't keep things separate. For the past nine years there was no problem keeping my secret, but the moment you followed me to Chicago and made that bid, all that changed."

He was serious. He really thought she was to blame for this situation. A part of Cris wanted to weep with the pain of that realization. Another part wanted to reach out and smack the taste out of Dylan's mouth.

She did neither.

"I'll speak to Garrett. He won't share those pictures with anyone, so you can stop worrying about that. I'm also going to take a few steps back from whatever this was that we were doing. I have a new career direction that I'm heading in and I'll need all my time and energy devoted to making that happen. I'm sure you can understand that."

Cris's fingers had been digging into the soft leather of her purse as she'd held it in front of her these past few minutes. Her chest felt tight, her cheeks were warm and damn those ridiculous tears threatened to fall at any minute. The very last thing Cris wanted was to cry over Dylan, and she especially did not want to do it in front of him. She took a slow steadying breath and mustered a smile.

"We were always able to be honest with each other about anything. I think that's what I was looking forward to most about returning to D.C. I thought I'd come back to my best friend and biggest supporter and would finally find a rewarding job that I could be proud of. If we finally decided to act on the desire that had been on a slow simmer between us years ago, cool beans." She gave a nervous chuckle, but a sob was burning in the back of her throat.

"I'm not too proud to admit when I'm wrong. And before you start to think that this has something to do with your sexual preference, let me stop you right there. What you do at the club, what you figured out you like, it isn't so bad, Dylan. You're not causing physical harm or disrespecting anyone. You're an adult and you spend your personal time with other consenting adults. As far as I'm concerned that's more commendable than what many other people out here are doing in what they deem "traditional" relationships. No, the situation you're grappling with right now doesn't even have much to do with Garrett and his antics. This is all about you. It's about the life you believe you've been ordained to have. It's about the resentment you still hold against your parents and your inability to actually live on your own terms, regardless of how you try to convince yourself otherwise. None of that has anything to do with me. So I'm going to step away and let you do what you do best, live your life the way you see fit. Even if that life keeps you and all that you could give and receive in a bottle filled with fear."

Cris wanted to say more. She wanted to say something that might possibly get through to him, but the tears wanted their freedom more. So she turned at that moment and walked as fast as she could without actually running out of his office. During her hasty dissent she heard Gwen call out to her but all she could do was shake her head and keep moving. She'd send the woman a card or something later just so she'd know that it wasn't anything personal. Thankfully the elevator came quickly and Cris was soon behind its closed doors. The first tear fell before she'd made it through the lobby of the building.

It was after eight that evening and Dylan was still in the office. He'd had a mountain of work to do.

But he hadn't done any of it.

Instead, he'd been troubleshooting and thinking. Lots of thinking.

For the first hour after Cris had stormed out of his office, Dylan remained rooted to that spot in front of his desk. His backside had grown sore from leaning on the edge of his desk, but he hadn't been able to move, not until he'd thought through every word that she'd said. That had taken him longer than he would have imagined because for the first time in his life a situation was not black and white or cut and dry. There was no clear answer, or any sound reasoning to lead him to a final resolution. All there was were emotions swirling and tangling inside of him causing the exact amount of havoc he always knew they would.

The ringing of his desk phone had interrupted him and Dylan returned to the other side of his desk. He did not answer the call, but let it roll over to Gwen's desk. Dylan knew his assistant had seen Cris leave in a hurry. He was also certain that Gwen would have picked up on how upset Cris was. When Gwen hadn't come into his office to find out what he'd done to Cris, immediately after Cris's departure, he knew she wouldn't. She was probably pissed off at him as well. Dylan had been doing a fine job of irritating the people he cared about most.

The next thing Dylan had done that afternoon was call The Corporation. Within the secret organization was a unit called The Cleaners. Dylan was transferred to a representative in that unit and reported his situation with Garrett. After writing the claim number and representative's name on a notepad, Dylan disconnected the call. Within the hour the representative would have a solution in play for how to get rid of those pictures and any future threat to their secret society. It was a perk to being a platinum member. There would be no physical harm done to anyone involved, but Garrett would be presented with an option that he could not refuse to delete all pictures and never entertain the idea of revealing the club or any of its members again.

As a secondary precaution, Dylan had called his father.

"Good to hear from you, son," Hanson said the moment his assistant had patched the call through to him.

"There's a situation I think you need to know about," Dylan had immediately begun.

There were no real formalities between Dylan and Hanson, no sentiments or emotional connections. It was the same with his mother, even though Demetria did insist that Dylan have dinner with her on her birthday and brunch with her and Hanson on Christmas Day if they were in town. That was as close to a family gathering as Dylan had ever experienced with his parents.

"What is it?" was Hanson's instant question.

Dylan had given an abbreviated version of the story, surprising himself by talking about his connection to an exclusive sex club with as much ease as he would have talked about current laws that needed to be changed.

"Well, that's a mess, but The Cleaners will handle it," Hanson replied.

"What did you just say?" Dylan hadn't mentioned anything about The Cleaners in his story. He'd only told his father that he had someone taking care of containment.

Hanson cleared his throat. "The Washington D.C. branch of The Corporation is one of the largest and most profitable in the country. In the last four years its membership has grown to come in second to Los Angeles's and was a few hundred over New York's."

Dylan had been rubbing a hand over his jaw while his temples throbbed. "And you're one of those members," he stated dryly. He did not want to think of his parents as members at The Corporation. And he definitely did not want to know if his father was going to the club alone.

"It's something to do," Hanson answered. "Now, your situation will be handled and I trust that you'll be more careful in the future."

The not-so-gentle chastisement rubbed over Dylan like a thick wool sweater, scratching his skin with irritation.

"I'll take care of myself and my business from now on."

"There's no need to get testy, Dylan. Every member pays for the protection The Corporation offers. It's a wonderful benefit. I've known others who have found themselves in sticky situations as a result of visiting the club. It happens. I'm just telling my son to be more careful in the future. I'm scheduled to formally announce my run for the presidency the first of the year and your mother is in the process of restructuring her company so that she'll be more available for the campaign. I expect you to do your part as well. I have plans to bring one of the youngest black partners at a prestigious D.C. firm on the campaign trail too."

That's exactly what Dylan was to him, the son of a senator turned presidential candidate. Never just his "son".

"I have to get back to work," Dylan had said and ended the call with the one man from whom he'd expected so much more.

Hours had passed after that call with Dylan still thinking,

contemplating every decision he'd ever made and the reason behind them. It all made him wonder if Cris had been right. Was he living his life in fear?

Now, Dylan's stomach growled and he looked up at the clock on his wall to see that it was ten minutes after eight. He'd skipped lunch and dinner. His cell phone rang and thoughts of food were lost as he saw the name and number on the screen.

"Hey, Mama Peaches," he answered.

"Hi, Dylan. I'm just checking on you. Want to find out how your date went?"

"The date was weeks ago," he told her. "But it went, um, okay." He didn't really know how to put into words how life-altering that date had been.

"You still seeing that pretty little lady? You know she sent me an email early this morning asking how the project was going. I thought that was real nice of her to keep in touch," Mama Peaches told him.

"Yes. It was," Dylan agreed but wasn't totally sure why Cris would have reached out to Mama Peaches. She had mentioned to him that she thought the project was a good idea which is why she had no problem donating, but Dylan was still shocked to hear that she'd sent Mama Peaches an email.

"She said she just relocated to D.C. so I was thinking that it would be good if you two could see more of each other."

"You don't even know her, Mama Peaches," Dylan said with a shake of his head. Even though he wondered if the woman had a sixth sense. How had she known to call at the exact time Dylan was contemplating what to do about Cris?

"Besides, I'm not into dating and relationships." That

declaration sounded hollow to his ears but Dylan couldn't take it back.

"You can get into anything you want, Dylan. I knew that after I found out about that 'ole club you went to."

"What?" This was not possible. "What club?"

"Remember when you came back for Harold's funeral? You and a few of my Gents stayed at the house with me. It was just like old times with you boys that week, except instead of y'all leaving tennis shoes and video games all around the house, you had your keys and cell phones scattered about. I was moving your keys and phone to put them near your coat one morning and I saw the card from a place called The Corporation. Took me and Geraldine a couple weeks to figure out what kinda place that was. But when we did I told Geraldine it was 'cause you were always so lonely. No matter how many people had lived in this house when you were here, you came alone and you left the same way. Poor chile."

Dylan was all set to be irritated that she knew he went to a club to pay for sex, until she'd said those last words. Her voice had changed to that of the woman who had wrapped her arms around him the first night he'd been in her house. Dylan hadn't wanted to be there in Chicago, but the problem was there was really no other place he longed to be because it wasn't like he'd had any real home to miss. But there'd been something about the way it felt being held in her arms and how she'd whispered to him, "Poor chile always being left behind. Well, you've got a home here with Mama Peaches, for as long as you want it."

Yes, he'd been a seventeen year-old boy at the time and shouldn't have needed a hug from some strange grandmotherly figure, but he'd never forgotten that night or how loved Mama Peaches had always made him feel.

"Now you listen to me, Dylan. Ain't nothing in that club gonna ever love you the way you deserve to be loved. And if that pretty little woman who paid all that money for one night with you isn't worthy of you, then so be it. But it's past time you got off your pity perch and opened your heart and mind to love. Harold and I had it for a real long time and that's the type of happiness I want for all of my boys."

Dylan didn't have a reply to that and it was seemingly okay, because Mama Peaches quickly hopped to another subject, telling him about the progress of the restoration project and a few legal snags they'd run into in the process. Before hanging up the phone Dylan thanked her, not only for saving him when he was a teenager, but also for inspiring him to fight for something now that he was an adult.

11

Two Weeks Later
South Carolina

*J*eremiah and Celestine Palmer may have lived what some in their town called an uppity life for a black family, but whenever they had a party they hired a band and a DJ who knew exactly when to play *Candy* by Cameo. At which time Celestine, who had seen *The Best Man* movie a kazillion times, would be first on the floor to start the electric slide. Tonight, Jeremiah followed his wife and so did a good portion of the one hundred and fifty guests who had come to celebrate Jeremiah's birthday.

Cris sat at the head table alone, because every member of her family was on the dance floor. She normally danced the night away at her parents' parties and celebrating her father's 60th birthday was definitely cause for celebration, but she just wasn't in the mood tonight. It had been two weeks since she'd seen or heard from Dylan. After leaving his office she'd taken a long walk to clear her mind and yes, to continue crying those foolish tears.

That was the moment when she detested everyone who'd ever warned friends not to become romantically involved. And likewise to those who said it was great to fall in love with their best friend. How could she have been so stupid?

Except Cris didn't think she'd been stupid at all. She was certain she hadn't misread the underlying desire in the relationship between her and Dylan. And she was even more positive that after the time they'd spent together in her hotel and at The Corporation that they'd grown closer. Dylan's anger and retreat should have also been foreseen, after all, she knew him very well. Dylan did not do relationships and commitment. He'd reminded her of that fact and she'd chosen to ignore him. That, she would take the heat for, but the rest—the fear that kept Dylan pulling away from her and any other real happiness in his life, she was laying that right at his feet.

As for Garrett's part in this scenario, Cris had tried to call and talk to him about those pictures. She'd actually planned to threaten him with the fact that she knew he and Tisha had cheated on the LSATs. If she sent a letter to the D.C. Bar with the proof she had of that—notes she'd found in the dorm room after Tisha had moved out their senior year- -they would definitely be disbarred. But by the time she'd gotten Garrett on the phone, he was already promising to never show the pictures and apologized profusely to Cris for even attempting the blackmail scheme. He'd also apologized for all the pain he'd caused her in the past and swore to never try to come on to her again. The entire conversation had been weird but Cris was glad that in the end Dylan, nor his father's job would be in danger because of those pictures.

After that, Cris had turned all her attention to working on her new project. She'd decided it was asinine not to use the money in her trust fund. It was silly to feel like she was taking a hand-out, when the money was hers to spend. With that in mind Cris had contacted a realtor and the minute she returned to D.C. she would start a search for a house to buy.

"Hey girl, you better get on up here and dance." Melissa Frank worked at Cris's father's insurance company. She was dancing close to the table where Cris was sitting.

"Maybe next song," Cris yelled back in response.

Probably not, she didn't really feel like dancing. She felt like spending even more of her time thinking, which is all it felt like she'd been doing for the last couple of weeks. That changed the moment Melissa hit a turn on the dance floor which allowed Cris to see the guy dancing on the other side of her.

Cris sat up in the chair her eyes glued to Dylan as he moved to the beat of the music in a way no other person on that dance floor was. Of course he was doing all the correct moves, it was just the way he was doing them. That plus how good he looked wearing dark blue jeans, a crisp white chambray shirt and chocolate brown suede shoes. His hair was neatly trimmed, his body looked even more toned than it had been just two weeks ago, and his smile...it took her breath away. Dylan hadn't smiled much in the weeks that she'd been back in D.C. Yes, he'd joked with her about their past and seemed to enjoy their time together, even when they weren't having sex, but he never smiled the way he was right now.

When he caught her staring at him, Dylan crocked a finger, beckoning her to join him on the floor. Cris wasn't in the mood for dancing, at least that's what she'd just told herself a few seconds ago, but now she was standing and walking toward Dylan before the dance took him on another turn. Once she was beside him, full of questions, Cris simply fell into step, moving along with the crowd. In seconds she was laughing and enjoying the feel of moving to the rhythm combined with the low buzz of energy starting to fizz between her and Dylan.

When the dance was over Dylan took Cris's hand and walked her off the floor and into the lobby of the country club where the party was being held.

"What are you doing here?" she asked the moment they stood off to a quiet corner.

"I came here to say some things to you," he started.

"Wait, if this is about what happened," she began. Cris was going to tell him that she didn't want to talk about it. She didn't want to rehash how he felt or why he felt it necessary to push her away. She actually didn't know what she wanted to hear from Dylan or how she should be reacting to him at this moment. All she knew was that he was here and looking damn sexy.

He touched a finger to her lips to stop her next words and Cris frowned up at him. Dylan pulled his fingers away.

"I'm sorry. It was necessary," he said. "I was wrong. I was mean and stupid."

Cris took a step back from him. She folded her arms over

her chest and tilted her head to stare and wait for him to continue.

"I wanted to push you away because a few months after you left for law school it finally started to make sense to me that it was normal for you to leave. My parents had spent a lifetime leaving me. Sure, they dragged me mostly everywhere they went, but with each trip, each time they chose business and their careers over me, they were actually leaving me. So I got used to that." He shrugged.

"I figured that's how my life was meant to be."

"It doesn't have to be," she told him, her voice a little scratchy because she wasn't prepared for the emotion welling up in her throat.

"I know. You showed me that. Coming back to D.C. and putting yourself right in my path no matter how hard I tried to skirt around you and what had been brewing between us for so long. You saved me, Cristine."

She shook her head. "But you didn't want to be saved."

"No," he said with a sigh. "I didn't. But I've had a lot of time to think about that and how it wasn't necessarily a bad thing. I've made some decisions in my business and personal life, but they're all contingent on you."

"What do you mean? How do your business decisions affect me?"

He stepped closer to her. With his finger he pushed back one of the loose curls that had fallen from her up-do while she was dancing.

"Because I cannot live without you."

Cris could only blink at him, words were temporarily lost.

"I could go on the way I was and so could you, but we

wouldn't be happy. We wouldn't be complete. We're more than best friends, Cris, we're two halves of a whole. And I need you in order to move forward with my life."

Seconds seemed like hours as her muteness continued.

"I love you, Cris."

Now Cris knew what she was supposed to say. She knew what she felt and how long she'd waited to hear those words from Dylan in a non-platonic way. But giving in easily was not in her nature. She stepped back from him once more.

"What decisions did you make concerning business that involve me?"

Dylan chuckled. "I should have known you'd make me grovel."

"Hell yeah, you deserve it after your sour attitude the last few weeks. Now tell me what's going on."

He stuffed his hands into his front pockets and nodded. "Okay, so remember you were trying to figure out why you didn't want the job as a transactional attorney?"

"Uh huh."

"Well, at the same time I was wondering why I'd become so intent on helping a neighborhood I'd never lived in become more viable. I told myself it was because I owed it to Mama Peaches. I mean, even though I only stayed with her for six months and this new project has nothing to do with the good work she's doing in Southlake. She has inspired so many aspects of my life and I owed her for being so kind to me for those six months, but that's not all. I realized that I owed it to myself to do something I could really be proud of, something that would help people that look like me."

"I don't understand where this is going."

"It's going to Chicago, with me. And hopefully you too. I want you to move to Chicago and open a law firm with me. A firm where we would offer assistance to not only the citizens in Century Heights, but anyone else who may not otherwise be able to afford legal services."

Cris could not believe it. Had he been snooping into her thoughts these past two weeks? "I decided I wanted to open my own firm, to take the cases that were important to me and that would help people, not just corporations. How did you know?"

He shrugged. "I didn't. I was actually hoping you wouldn't get angry at me for being presumptuous and making these plans without consulting with you first."

"But you are consulting with me now, right? You haven't actually opened your own firm yet?"

"No. I'd like it to be a partnership."

She smiled and said, "Palmer and James LLP. I like the sound of that."

Dylan shook his head. "James and James," he told her. "I'm asking you to be my business and lifetime partner."

Cris could only shake her head at first, then those pesky little tears that she swore only wanted to make an appearance for Dylan, showed up again.

"I think I've loved you forever," she admitted.

Dylan came close to her again. He cupped her face in his hands this time and kissed her lips softly, "Good because I'd rather not think of you placing a bid on anyone else for the rest of our lives."

"Not a chance," she whispered and wrapped her arms around his neck. "You were the first, the last and the only lover I would ever bid on, Dylan James."

"That's good to hear, future Mrs. Cristine James."

Dylan didn't wait for a response from her this time, his lips were on hers once more and by joining in that kiss, Cris's answer was given.

ALSO BY AC ARTHUR

CONTEMPORARY ROMANCE—SERIES AND SINGLE
TITLES BY AC ARTHUR

**The Donovan Series, Donovan Friends, & Donovan
Dynasty books (in reading order)**

The Carrington Chronicles

Book 1: WANTING YOU - Part One

Book 2: WANTING YOU - Part Two

Book 3: NEEDING YOU

Book 4: HAVING YOU

* * *

The Rumors Series

Book 1: RUMORS

Book 2: REVEALED

* * *

The Royal Weddings

Book 1: TO MARRY A PRINCE

Book 2: LOVING THE PRINCESS

Book 3: PRINCE EVER AFTER

Book 4: TAMING THE PRINCE

* * *

The Temptation Series

Book 1: ONE MISTLETOE WISH

Book 2: ONE UNFORGETTABLE KISS

Book 3: ONE PERFECT MOMENT

Book 4: ONE CHRISTMAS SONG

* * *

Fashion & Passion

Book 1: A PRIVATE AFFAIR (Coming 2019)

Book 2: AT YOUR SERVICE (Coming 2020)

* * *

OBJECT OF HIS DESIRE

UNCONDITIONAL

LOVE ME CAREFULLY

HEART OF THE PHOENIX

SECOND CHANCE, BABY

SING YOUR PLEASURE

DECADENT DREAMS

EVE OF PASSION

CONTEMPORARY SMALL TOWN ROMANCE (W/A
LACEY BAKER)

The Sweetland Series

Book 1: HOMECOMING

Book 2: JUST LIKE HEAVEN

Book 3: SUMMER'S MOON

* * *

A GINGERBREAD ROMANCE (Coming Oct 2019)

SEXY PARANORMAL ROMANCE

The Shadow Shifters (in reading order)

Book 1: TEMPTATION RISING

Book 2: SEDUCTION'S SHIFT

Book 3: PASSION'S PREY

* * *

The Damaged Hearts Series

(Shadow Shifters Spinoff)

Book 1: MINE TO CLAIM

Book 2: PART OF ME

Book 3: HUNGER FOR YOU

Book 1-3: DAMAGED HEARTS BOX SET

* * *

Book 4: SHIFTER'S CLAIM

Book 5: HUNGER'S MATE

Book 6: PRIMAL HEAT

Book 7: A LION'S HEART

* * *

The Wolf Mates

The Alpha's Woman (Available as part of the GROWL
Anthology and CLAIMED BY THE MATE VOL. 1 Duology)

Her Perfect Mates (Available as part of the WILD Anthology and CLAIMED BY THE MATE VOL. 2 Duology)

Bound to the Wolf (Available as part of the HUNGER Anthology
and CLAIMED BY THE MATE VOL. 3 Duology)

* * *

The Legion

Book 1: AWAKEN THE DRAGON (November 2019)

YOUNG ADULT PARANORMAL (W/A ARTIST ARTHUR)

The Mystyx Series

Book 1: MANIFEST

Book 2: MYSTIFY

Book 3: MAYHEM

A Mystyx Novella: MUTINY

Book 4: MESMERIZE

ABOUT THE AUTHOR

Stay in touch with A.C. on the web!

Be the first to know when A.C. Arthur's next book is available!
Follow her at BookBub to get an alert whenever she has a new
release, preorder, or discount!
www.bookbub.com/profile/a-c-arthur

Visit the "Contact" page on her website, www.acarthur.net, to
sign up for her monthly newsletter.

"Follow", "Friend" and/or "Like" her on Facebook (AC
Arthur's Book Lounge), Twitter (@ACArthur), Pinterest
(acarthur22), Instagram (@acarthurbooks), Tumblr
(acarthurbooks), Google Plus and GoodReads.

54696015R00078

Made in the USA
Columbia, SC
04 April 2019